THE BLOODFIRE CURSE

LADY HEARTSWELL

CENTURIA BOOKS LLC

CONTENTS

Chapter One

SHADOWS AT THE THROAT

The rain tasted like iron and ash, a fitting flavor for a suicide mission.

I clung to the slick gargoyle jutting from the side of the Storm Citadel, my boots finding purchase on stone slippery enough to send a lesser climber to a shattered death three hundred feet below. Lightning cracked, turning the night sky into a fractured mirror of white and violet. For a second, the sprawling fortress was illuminated—towers like jagged teeth biting into the heavens, walls thick enough to hold back an army of giants.

Or one very small, very motivated woman from the Lower Wards.

My fingers ached. The cold had long since seeped through my leathers, settling into the marrow of my bones, but I didn't shiver. Shivering made you slip. Slipping meant death. And I couldn't die until the obsidian dagger strapped to my thigh was buried to the hilt in General Valdus's chest.

I pulled myself up, muscle by burning muscle, until I vaulted over the parapet and landed in a crouch. Silence wrapped around me instantly. I wasn't just quiet; I was a void in the air.

The plan was simple. Stupid, but simple. Infiltrate the dragon keep. Find the High Commander's quarters. End the monster who had turned my city into a labor camp for his war machine.

A heavy, wet sound echoed from the courtyard below the ramparts. A whimper.

I froze. That wasn't a human sound.

My objective lay to the north, up the winding stairs to the Commander's spire. But the sound came again—a high-pitched, gurgling cry of pain, followed by the wet *thwack* of leather hitting flesh.

Ignore it, Vea.

I took a step toward the spire.

Another cry. This one broke into a screech that grated against my ribs.

"Shut it up before the Commander hears," a gruff voice growled. "Filthy beast."

My feet stopped. I looked down into the recessed stable yard. Three guards in the blackened armor of the Sky Legion stood in a circle. They weren't patrolling. They were entertained.

In the center of the mud, chained to a post with links heavy enough to anchor a ship, was a wyvern hatchling. It couldn't have been more than a few months old—its scales were still soft, a mottled grey that hadn't hardened into armor yet. Its wing was bent at a sickening angle.

One of the guards, a man with a beard like steel wool, winded up a heavy coil of rope and brought it down. The hatchling shrieked, fireless smoke puffing from its nostrils as it tried to scramble away, but the chains held it fast.

"tough leather," the second guard laughed, taking a swig from a flask. "Make good boots."

My hand hovered over the hilt of my dagger.

This is not the mission. Valdus was the target. Valdus was the disease; these men were just the symptoms. If I engaged, I risked noise. I risked the alarm. I risked the only chance my people had at freedom.

The hatchling looked up. Its eyes were wide, reptilian saucers of terror, reflecting the torchlight. It didn't look like a monster. It looked like me when I was six years old, cornered in an alley with nothing but a rusted spoon to defend myself.

The guard raised the rope again. "Let's see if it bleeds black."

The decision hit me before my brain authorized it.

I dropped from the wall.

Falling twenty feet was nothing. I rolled upon impact, the mud silencing the thud, and sprang up like a compressed spring released. The dagger was in my hand before I finished the motion.

The bearded guard never saw me. I slammed the pommel of my blade into the base of his skull. Bone crunched. He folded like wet laundry.

The second guard dropped his flask. "What the—"

I didn't let him finish. I swept his legs, using my low center of gravity to upend him. He hit the mud with a splash. I was on him instantly, a knee to his throat to crush the air from his windpipe.

"Intruder!" the third guard bellowed, fumbling for the sword at his hip.

Too slow. I launched myself off the gasping man on the ground, twisting in the air. I was small—barely five feet of malice and scar tissue—but I used that. I was a projectile. I slammed into the third guard's chest, driving him back into the stone wall. My forearm pressed against his windpipe, the tip of my obsidian blade hovering over his eye.

"Drop it," I hissed. My voice was gravel and smoke.

The sword clattered to the stones.

Silence returned to the courtyard, heavy and suffocating, broken only by the ragged breathing of the men on the ground and the soft mewling of the wyvern.

I stepped back, chest heaving. My cover was blown. The shout would bring others. I had to move. I had to kill them or run, and I didn't have the stomach to slit the throats of unconscious drunkards.

I turned to the hatchling. It flinched, cowering against the post.

"I'm not going to hurt you," I whispered, reaching for the heavy iron lock on its collar. My hands were shaking. Not from fear, but from the adrenaline crash. I picked the lock with the tip of my dagger—a trick learned in the gutters of the Lower Wards.

The lock clicked. The chains fell away.

"Go," I urged. "Fly, you idiot."

The creature didn't move. It stared past me, its pupils contracting into slits. It wasn't looking at freedom. It was looking at the archway behind me.

The air in the courtyard changed. The temperature didn't drop; it vanished, replaced by a pressure that made my ears pop. The rain seemed to slow down.

The hairs on my arms stood up, electrically charged.

I turned slowly.

Standing in the archway was a shadow darker than the night.

General Valdus.

The posters in the city didn't do him justice. They depicted a man. This was not a man. This was a force of nature wrapped in black leather and midnight steel. He filled the archway, his shoulders broad enough to carry the collapse of the sky.

He didn't hold a weapon. He didn't need one.

He stepped into the light of the torches, and the air rushed out of my lungs.

He was terrifying. He was beautiful.

He was big in a way that felt predatory, a towering expanse of hard muscle and lethal grace. Rain plastered his dark curls to his forehead, water dripping down a face carved from granite. High cheekbones, a jawline sharp enough to cut glass, and a mouth currently set in a line of bored cruelty.

But it was the rest of him that made my mouth go dry.

He wore a sleeveless training tunic, wet and clinging to his torso like a second skin. It left nothing to the imagination. The fabric strained over the slabs of his chest, outlining abdominals that looked like cobblestones. His arms were tree trunks, roped with veins and corded muscle that shifted with every subtle movement. Scars silvered his tan skin—a map of violence that marked him as a survivor of a thousand wars.

My gaze dropped to his hands. They were massive. Hands that could crush a skull as easily as they could crush a grape. Hands that could snap me in half without trembling.

Heat, sharp and humiliating, spiked low in my belly. *Stop it.* He is the enemy. He is the monster.

His eyes—molten, burning gold—swept over the scene. They touched the unconscious guards, the mud, the blood. They didn't even flicker.

Then they landed on the hatchling.

The terrifying stillness of him broke. He moved, not toward me, but toward the creature. He didn't walk; he prowled, a apex predator acknowledging a lesser beast.

I gripped my dagger, knuckles white. This was my chance. His back was to me. I could drive the blade between his ribs.

But I couldn't move. My feet were nailed to the mud.

Valdus knelt in the muck. He didn't care about the pristine leather of his breeches. He reached out a hand—those massive, deadly fingers—and the hatchling didn't recoil. It leaned in.

"Easy," he murmured. His voice was a deep rumble that vibrated through the stones and straight into my chest. "They hurt you?"

The wyvern chirped, pressing its snout against his palm.

Valdus examined the bent wing with a tenderness that unmoored me. His touch was gentle, reverent. Golden light flared softly from his fingertips—magic, warm and healing. The hatchling let out a sigh of relief as the bones knit back together under his ministrations.

"You're safe," Valdus said, his voice dropping an octave, thick with a strange, possessive warmth. "Go to the aerie. Rest."

The hatchling nudged him one last time, then scrambled back, testing its healed wing before launching itself into the rainy sky.

Valdus watched it go. For a second, the monster was gone. In his place was something else—something weary and strangely protective. Something that made the ache in my chest flare hotter.

Then he stood up.

And the monster returned.

He turned slowly, pivoting on his heel to face me. The golden warmth vanished from his eyes, replaced by a glacial, bored indifference.

He looked at me. Not *at* me, but *through* me. Like I was a smudge of dirt on his boot.

"You," he said. One word. A judgment.

I raised my dagger, shifting into a defensive stance. "General."

He didn't draw a weapon. He didn't even raise his hands. He just walked toward me.

"Stay back," I warned, feinting a lunge.

He didn't break stride.

I struck. I was fast—faster than the guards. My blade arc for the unprotected skin of his throat.

He caught my wrist.

He didn't block. He didn't dodge. He just... caught me.

The impact jarred my teeth. His grip was iron. Immovable. Absolute. He stopped my momentum dead, halting a strike that would have felled an ox.

His skin was burning hot.

"Fast," he noted, his voice devoid of praise. "For a rat."

I twisted, trying to kick his knee, but he anticipated the movement. He jerked my arm, spinning me around and slamming my back against his chest.

The air left me in a rush. I was enveloped by him—the scent of ozone, rain, and sandalwood. His body was a wall of hard, unyielding heat against my spine. I was trapped.

His free hand—the one that had just healed a broken wing with gentle magic—wrapped around my throat.

He lifted.

My feet left the ground.

Panic flared, cold and sharp. I clawed at his forearm, my nails digging into his skin, but it was like clawing at stone. He held me suspended in the air, my boots dangling a foot above the mud.

He turned me around so I was facing him. Up close, his eyes were terrifying. Swirls of gold and black, ancient and devoid of humanity.

He squeezed. Not enough to kill. Just enough to remind me that my life existed only because he allowed it.

"Did you think," he murmured, his face inches from mine, "that killing three drunkards authorized you to stand in my presence?"

I gasped for air, staring defiantly into that golden abyss. "They... were hurting... it."

Something flickered in his gaze. Surprise? No. Annoyance.

He tilted his head, studying me. His thumb traced the line of my jaw, rough and calloused. The touch burned. It shouldn't have felt like that. It should have been painful, violating. Instead, a jolt of electricity arced from his skin to mine, racing down my nerves and settling heavy between my thighs.

My body betrayed me. My heart hammered a traitorous rhythm against my ribs.

"You're small," he said, as if stating a fact about the weather. "Frail. A gutter rat wrapped in stolen leather."

"I'll... kill... you," I choked out.

His mouth curved. It wasn't a smile. It was a baring of teeth.

"You can't even breathe without my permission, Little Red."

He tightened his grip, cutting off the world for a split second. darkness fringed my vision.

Then, he released me.

He didn't set me down. He tossed me.

I flew backward, landing hard in the mud, skidding a few feet. I gasped, sucking in greedy lungfuls of wet air, coughing as the rain plastered my hair to my face.

I scrambled to my knees, searching for my dagger. It lay in the muck near his boot.

Valdus kicked it away. It Skittered across the stones, disappearing into a drain.

He looked down at me, his expression one of utter disdain. He wiped his hand on his breeches, as if touching me had soiled him.

"The guards will wake in five minutes," he said, turning his back to me. "If you are still here, I will feed you to the thing you just saved."

He began to walk away, toward the castle doors.

"Why?" I screamed, the word tearing from my raw throat. "Why let me go?"

He paused, glancing over his shoulder. The look he gave me withered my soul. It wasn't anger. It wasn't hate.

It was indifference.

"I don't kill insects," he said. "I step on them. And tonight, I don't want to clean my boots."

The heavy oak doors slammed shut behind him, the sound echoing like a thunderclap.

I sat alone in the mud, shivering violently. Not from the cold. Not from the fear.

But from the terrifying realization that when his hand had been on my throat, when his heat had engulfed me, I hadn't wanted him to let go.

I looked at the closed doors. The monster had spared me.

He would regret it.

I pushed myself up, my legs trembling. I had failed. I had lost my weapon. I had been humiliated.

But I was still alive.

"Next time, Valdus," I whispered to the rain, wiping the mud from my face. "Next time, you won't see the insect coming until it stings."

I turned and ran into the shadows, the phantom pressure of his fingers still burning a brand into my skin.

Chapter Two

A Tether of Shadow and Steel

The storm outside battered the stone walls of the Storm Citadel, but inside the High Commander's quarters, the silence was absolute.

I clung to the shadows of the vaulted ceiling, wedged between a heavy oak beam and the rough-hewn stone. My clothes were still sodden, sticking to my skin like a cold, wet shroud. My muscles screamed in protest, locked tight to keep me from shivering. Shivering made noise. Noise meant death.

Below me, the room was a cavern of dark luxury. Black iron, obsidian statues, and furs thick enough to swallow a person whole. A fire crackled in the grate, casting long, dancing shadows that did little to warm the ice in my veins.

General Valdus stood by the hearth.

He had stripped off his wet leather armor. Now, he wore only loose black trousers that hung low on his hips. The firelight licked across the expanse of his back—a monument of violence carved from scarred skin and corded muscle. A tattoo of a dragon in mid-flight stretched across his shoulder blades, the ink so dark it seemed to absorb the light.

He poured a drink from a crystal decanter. Amber liquid splashed into a heavy glass.

I shifted my grip on the dagger. This was madness. He had spared me once tonight, tossing me aside like refuse. Inspecting me like a bug before deciding I wasn't worth the squashed mess on his boot. That indifference burned hotter than hate.

I would not be an insect. I would be the end of him.

He took a sip, the movement slow, deliberate.

" The rafters are dusty, Little Red," he said.

His voice was a low rumble, carrying effortlessly to my perch. He hadn't turned around. He hadn't even looked up.

My heart slammed against my ribs, a trapped bird battering a cage.

"You breathe too loud," he added, swirling his drink. "And you smell like the sewers."

Stealth was gone. Only violence remained.

I dropped.

I didn't aim for the floor. I aimed for his back. Gravity was my only ally against a creature of his size. I fell through the air, dagger leading, a scream of rage locked behind my teeth.

He moved with a speed that defied physics.

One moment he was facing the fire; the next, he had spun, the glass in his hand shattering on the hearth.

I expected him to block. I expected him to dodge.

He did neither.

He caught me out of the air.

His hand—massive and searing hot—snapped around my throat. The momentum of my fall should have knocked him backward. Instead, he absorbed the impact like a stone wall, his boots not even shifting on the rug.

My spine jarred as he slammed me down onto the heavy oak table in the center of the room. Wood groaned under the impact.

Air fled my lungs. Stars exploded behind my eyes.

"Persistent," he growled, leaning over me.

I didn't waste time gasping. I slashed.

My dagger, still clutched in my right hand, arced toward his face. He caught my wrist mid-swing, his grip crushing the delicate bones. But he was a fraction too slow, or perhaps he just didn't care.

The obsidian blade bit into the meat of his palm.

It wasn't a deep cut, just a graze, but it was enough.

My blood from the earlier scrape on my arm smeared against his open wound. Red mixed with red.

The world ended.

It didn't fade to black. It dissolved into white. A sound roared through the room—not a noise, but a pressure, a thunderclap of silence that sucked the oxygen from the air and imploded the windows.

Glass shattered inward. The fire in the grate turned an impossible, blinding violet.

A shockwave blasted outward from where our skin touched. The table beneath me cracked down the center with the sound of a pistol shot.

My dagger flew from my numb fingers, clattering uselessly across the floor.

But I couldn't watch it go. I couldn't look away from him.

Something snapped in the center of my chest. A tether. A hook. A chain forged of pure, molten gravity slammed into my soul and anchored itself to the man looming over me.

Pain ripped through me—not physical, but existential. It was a violation. A door inside me, one I hadn't known existed, was kicked open, and *he* flooded in.

I felt his shock, a jagged spike of cold. I felt his rage, a burning inferno. And beneath it all, I felt a terrifying, ancient hunger that wasn't mine.

Mine.

The word wasn't spoken. It vibrated in the marrow of my bones.

Valdus froze. His pupils blew wide, swallowing the gold until his eyes were two pools of endless night. The veins in his neck corded, pulsing with a rhythm that matched the frantic, heavy thudding of my own heart.

He didn't pull away. He couldn't.

The air in the room grew heavy, thick as syrup. The magic coiled around us, a tangible thing, tasting of ozone and blood-iron. It purred in my veins, a sickening, seductive vibration that commanded me to *submit*, to *yield*, to *stay*.

I hated it. I hated him.

"What..." I gasped, the word scrapping my throat. "What did you do to me?"

Valdus stared down at me, his face a mask of absolute horror. The hand on my throat loosened, but he didn't let go. His thumb brushed the pulse point fluttering wildly beneath my jaw.

"Carrix," he whispered. The word sounded like a curse.

Heat flared in his palm where my blade had cut him. It traveled up his arm, golden light tracing his veins like liquid fire, jumping from his skin to mine where he held me. It burned. It felt like branding iron and ice all at once.

"Get off," I snarled, panic making my limbs thrash.

I tried to kick him. I tried to buck him off.

He didn't budge. He weighed three hundred pounds of solid muscle, and right now, he felt like a mountain settling on top of me.

The movement seemed to snap the paralysis holding him. His eyes narrowed, the shock bleeding away into something darker. Something predatory.

He lowered his head.

"No," I choked out.

He didn't listen. The bond—that terrible, golden chain—yanked him down.

He buried his face in the crook of my neck.

He inhaled deeply. The sound was wet, animalistic. He was scenting me. Hunting for the truth of what the magic was screaming at him.

His nose brushed my skin, and a jolt of pleasure, sharp and unwanted, spiked through my belly. It was a betrayal of the highest order. My body arched into him before my mind could scream a protest.

"Strawberries," he murmured against my skin, his voice rough with confusion and need. "And steel."

"Let me go!" I drove my knee up, aiming for his groin.

He caught my leg with his free hand, pinning it to the table. Now I was splayed open beneath him, completely at his mercy.

He lifted his head. His eyes were glowing—literally glowing—with an inner, molten light. The human mask was gone. The dragon was looking at me.

"I cannot let you go," he said. The resignation in his tone terrified me more than his anger ever could. "If I let you go, I will hunt you down before you reach the door."

"I'll kill you," I promised, though my voice trembled. "I will rip your throat out."

His gaze dropped to my mouth.

The air between us crackled, charged with enough energy to power a city. The hatred in my chest warred with the magnetic pull of the bond. It wanted me to touch him. It wanted me to crawl inside his skin.

"Try," he challenged.

He crashed his mouth to mine.

It wasn't a kiss. It was a collision. A claiming.

His lips were hard, unyielding, bruising mine with a desperation that tasted of ash and violence. There was no tenderness, no romance. It was a biological imperative, a predator marking his territory.

He tasted like whiskey and ruin.

I should have bitten him. I should have fought.

But the moment our mouths met, the roaring in my ears stopped. The pain in my chest eased, replaced by a terrifying sense of *rightness*. The magic surged, joyous and golden, welding the broken pieces of my soul to his.

My hands, traitors that they were, fisted in the loose fabric of his trousers. I wasn't pushing him away. I was pulling him closer.

He groaned, a low vibration against my lips, and deepened the kiss. His tongue swept into my mouth, arrogant and demanding, stealing my breath, my will, my sanity.

For a second, I forgot he was the monster who burned villages. I forgot I was an assassin. I was just a woman drowning in fire, and he was the only solid thing in the universe.

Then, reality returned with the force of a hammer.

He is the enemy.

I clamped my teeth down on his lower lip. Hard.

Iron tang of blood filled my mouth.

Valdus jerked back, a growl ripping from his chest. He touched his lip, his fingers coming away red.

He didn't look angry. He looked... wrecked. His chest heaved, his golden eyes wide and blown.

He looked at the blood on his fingers, then at me.

"You have no idea what you've done," he whispered.

The door to the chamber burst open.

"General!" A voice shouted. "The explosion—we saw the light—"

Valdus moved instantly. The languid predator was gone, replaced by the Commander.

He grabbed a fur throw from the back of the broken chair and threw it over me, bundling me up until only my face was visible. He hauled me off the table, tucking me against his side like a parcel.

"Get out!" Valdus roared at the guards standing in the doorway.

The soldiers flinched, eyes darting from the shattered windows to the cracked table, and finally to the small, bundled form tucked under the General's massive arm.

"Sir, is that... is that the assassin?" one guard asked, hand on his sword.

Valdus looked down at me. His grip on my waist was tight enough to bruise. The bond hummed between us, a live wire of panic and possession. He couldn't let them take me. If they took me, they would kill me.

And if I died... the sudden, hollow ache in his chest told me he would die too.

"No," Valdus lied, his voice cold as the grave. "This is my new prisoner. Prepare the Black Cell."

" The dungeon?" the guard asked, confused. "Sir, standard protocol is execution."

"I said the dungeon!" Valdus bellowed. The room shook. "And if anyone touches her, I will flay the skin from their bones."

He didn't wait for a response. He turned and dragged me toward the hidden service entrance behind the hearth.

I struggled against his grip, but I was exhausted, the magic having drained me dry.

"Where are you taking me?" I hissed into his chest.

He looked down, his jaw set in a line of grim determination.

"Somewhere no one can find you," he muttered. "Because if the King finds out what you are to me, he will burn us both."

"What am I to you?" I demanded.

Valdus stopped at the top of the dark stairwell. He looked at me, and for the first time, I saw genuine fear in the monster's eyes.

"You are the end of my world, Little Red."

He opened the door and pulled me into the dark.

Chapter Three

BURNING THE WORLD FOR A TASTE

The door to the secret passage slammed shut, plunging us into a darkness so heavy it felt like a physical weight.

Valdus didn't stop. His hand was a manacle around my upper arm, his grip bruising as he hauled me down the narrow, spiraling stone steps. The air here was stale, tasting of old dust and dry rot, a sharp contrast to the rain-slicked violence of the courtyard.

My boots skidded on the uneven stone. "Slow down!"

He ignored me. He moved with the terrifying, single-minded focus of a landslide. Every step he took vibrated through the floor and up my legs. The magical tether binding us—that golden, serrated chain forged in my own blood—yanked at my chest with every foot of distance I tried to put between us. It wasn't just a pull; it was a command. *Closer.*

I dug my heels in. I was small, but I was dense, a center of gravity low enough to anchor against the pull.

He hit the end of the slack and stopped. The sudden halt nearly dislocated my shoulder.

Valdus turned. In the gloom, the only light came from the faint, molten glow of his eyes. They weren't human. They were the eyes of a beast looking at its next meal, or perhaps its only lifeline.

"Do not fight me, Vea," he rasped. The name sounded foreign on his tongue, a curse he was trying to spit out.

"Let go of me, you oversized lizard." I clawed at his fingers. It was like trying to pry open a bear trap.

He didn't let go. He did the opposite.

He lunged.

Before I could draw a breath, he slammed me back against the rough-hewn wall of the stairwell. The stone bit into my spine, but the pain was instantly eclipsed by the wall of heat that was General Valdus.

He pinned me there, his body pressing mine into the rock. He was too big for the narrow space, too big for the world, a suffocating expanse of hard muscle and violence. His free hand planted against the wall by my head, boxing me in, while his thigh drove between my legs, pinning me in place.

The contact sent a shockwave of golden fire through my veins. My knees buckled. Only his body kept me upright.

"What is this?" I gasped, the air squeezed from my lungs. "What did you do?"

"I didn't do this," he growled, lowering his head until his nose brushed the shell of my ear. "You did this. You put your steel in my skin."

He inhaled. A long, dragging breath that shuddered through his massive frame.

The sound of it—that wet, desperate intake of air—sent a spike of heat straight to my groin. It was humiliating. I was an assassin. I was a weapon. I wasn't supposed to melt because the enemy was close enough to share my oxygen.

But the enemy looked like *this*.

My gaze traitorously raked over him in the dim light. Up close, the brutal reality of his size was overwhelming. He was a landscape of devastation. The damp linen of his shirt had gone translucent, clinging to a chest that looked like it had been chiseled from obsidian. Every breath he took strained the fabric, outlining the deep groove of his spine and the thick cables of muscle fastening his neck to shoulders broad enough to eclipse the sun. Pulse points hammered at his throat, frantic and heavy, betraying the icy control on his face. He was terrifyingly male, a concentrated dose of testosterone and lethal power that made every primitive instinct in my brain scream *mate*.

I wanted to run. I wanted to lick the sweat off his collarbone.

"You smell like rain," he murmured, his voice dropping to a subsonic rumble that vibrated in my teeth. "And blood. And trouble."

"Get off me," I whispered. It lacked conviction. My hands, instead of pushing him away, hovered over the damp fabric of his shirt, aching to touch the heat beneath.

"I can't." The admission was torn from him. "The bond... it wants to be fed."

He lifted his head. The gold in his irises had burned down to a smoky ring around pupils that were blown wide, black holes swallowing the light. He looked wrecked. He looked hungry.

"Fed?" I choked out.

"It thinks you belong to me."

He didn't give me time to process the horror of that statement.

His hand left the wall and tangled in my wet hair, wrenching my head back. It wasn't gentle. It was a demand for access.

Valdus crashed his mouth down on mine.

It wasn't a kiss. It was a collision of high-velocity desperate needs. His lips were hard, hot, and punishing. There was no romance in the way he devoured me; it was the frantic, starving graze of a man who had been holding his breath for a century and just found air.

I should have kneed him. I should have reached for the hidden blade in my boot.

Instead, I opened for him.

The moment our tongues met, the world dissolved. The cold, damp stairwell vanished. There was only fire. The bond snapped taut, humming a low, resonant note of absolute satisfaction. He tasted of brandy and raw power, a flavor that was addictive instantly.

His hand tightened in my hair, tilting my head to deepen the angle, devouring a groan that rose in my throat. His other arm, the one pinning me, wrapped around my waist, hauling me up until my feet dangled. He crushed me against the hard ridges of his armor-like chest, trying to merge our skeletons.

It was too much. It was overpowering. He was consuming me, burning through my defenses with the efficiency of a forest fire.

I was going to die here. Kissed to death by a dragon in a dark stairwell.

No.

He was the General. He was the man who burned the rebellion.

panic clawed its way through the haze of lust. I couldn't breathe. I couldn't think.

I snapped my teeth shut.

I bit his lower lip, hard enough to tear skin.

Valdus jerked back with a snarl, the sound animalistic and dangerous. He released me so suddenly I nearly crumpled to the stones.

He touched his mouth. His fingers came away smeared with bright red blood.

For a second, I thought he would kill me. The violence in the air was sharp enough to cut skin. His chest heaved, his jaw working as he fought for control. The golden light under his skin flared, pulsing in time with his heart, illuminating the jagged scar running down his cheek.

"You bit me," he said, his voice flat, dangerously calm.

I wiped my mouth, my hand trembling. "Touch me again, and I'll take the tongue next time."

He stared at me, the blackness in his eyes slowly receding, replaced by the cold, hard gold of the High Commander. He licked the blood from his lip, his gaze never leaving mine.

"If I wanted to hurt you, Little Red," he said softly, "you would already be ash."

He straightened, the predator retreating behind the mask of the general. He adjusted his cuffs, though his hands were shaking slightly.

"Get up," he ordered. "before I lose my temper again."

"Where are we going?" I demanded, pushing myself off the wall. My legs felt like water. My lips throbbed where his stubble had scraped them raw.

"Somewhere the King won't look for a dead assassin."

He turned and continued down the stairs. He didn't grab me this time. He didn't need to. The invisible chain between us was shorter now, tighter. If I stayed behind, the pain would cripple me.

I followed him into the dark.

*

The stairs ended in a heavy iron door that groaned in protest as Valdus shoved it open.

We stepped into a corridor lined with cells. This wasn't the common dungeon where drunks and thieves rotted. This was the Black Hold. The place where political prisoners and high-threat targets disappeared. The air was colder here, dry and smelling of ozone and despair.

Valdus marched past empty cells, his boots echoing on the flagstones. He stopped at the very end of the hall, before a door made not of bars, but of solid black iron bound with silver runes.

He placed his palm against the metal. The runes flared violet. The lock clicked with a sound like a breaking bone.

He swung the door open and gestured inside.

I peered into the gloom. It wasn't a hole in the ground. A narrow bed sat in the corner, covered in decent furs. A small table. A wash basin. No windows.

"Inside," he commanded.

I hesitated on the threshold. "You're locking me up."

"I am hiding you," he corrected, his voice tight. "The Citadel is crawling with the King's Inquisitors. If they find you, they will torture you to find out who sent you. And then they will execute you publicly."

"I'd prefer that to being your pet," I spat.

Valdus stepped closer, forcing me back into the cell. He loomed in the doorway, filling the frame, blocking out the only exit.

"You are not a pet," he said, his voice dropping to a whisper that scraped over my nerves. "You are a liability. A weakness I cannot afford."

"Then let me go."

"I can't." He looked at his hand, the one I had sliced, the one that had held me against the wall. The wound had already closed, leaving a faint silvery line. "The bond doesn't allow distance. If you leave the Citadel, I will hunt you. If you die..."

He stopped. A muscle feathered in his jaw.

"What?" I stepped closer, emboldened by his hesitation. "What happens if I die, Valdus?"

He looked at me then, and the raw vulnerability in his expression terrified me. It was a crack in the armor of a god.

"If you die, the fire in my blood will consume me," he said. "I will go mad. And in my madness, I will burn this kingdom until there is nothing left but glass."

The silence that followed was heavy, suffocating.

"So," he continued, stepping back and gripping the iron handle of the door. "You stay here. You stay alive. And you pray that I can find a way to break this before I decide you're not worth the risk."

"Valdus—"

He slammed the door.

The sound rang like a funeral bell. The runes flared once, then died, sealing me in.

I was alone.

I sank onto the narrow bed, my heart hammering a frantic rhythm against my ribs. I touched my lips. They still burned from his mouth. I could still taste him—blood and whiskey and ruin.

I hated him. I hated him for capturing me. I hated him for the things his soldiers had done to my city.

But as the silence of the Black Hold settled around me, the most terrifying thought wasn't that I was a prisoner.

It was that when he had kissed me, for one blinding, treacherous second, I hadn't been thinking about my dagger. I had been thinking about how much I wanted to burn with him.

I curled my knees to my chest, burying my face in my arms.

The monster had me. And I had a terrible feeling he wasn't the only one in danger.

CHAPTER FOUR

THE EDGE OF HIS RESTRAINT

I woke to the smell of lavender and lies.

My body tensed before my eyes opened, muscles coiled for the cold bite of stone or the rattle of iron chains. The dungeon floor should have been digging into my hip. The air should have tasted of mildew and rat droppings.

Instead, I lay on softness that felt like a sin.

Velvet. Silk. A mattress thick enough to drown in.

I sat up, the movement jarring a dull ache behind my eyes. This wasn't a cell. It was a cage gilded in gold. Tapestries made of heavy midnight-blue wool covered the stone walls, dampening the sound of the storm still raging outside. A fire burned in a hearth of black marble, the flames too steady, too perfect—magical fire, devoid of smoke.

I swung my legs over the edge of the bed. I was still in my leathers, but my boots had been removed. They sat by the door, upright and mocking.

"You slept for twelve hours."

The voice came from the shadows in the corner.

General Valdus.

My heart didn't just beat; it slammed against my ribs, a traitorous gong announcing my fear. He sat in a high-backed chair, one leg crossed over the other, looking like a king on a throne of darkness. He had changed. Gone were the wet breeches and the raw vulnerability of the stairwell. He wore a crisp black tunic embroidered with the silver dragon of the Sky Legion, the collar high and stiff against his throat.

He looked impeccable. Unreachable.

And the sight of him made my blood sing.

It was a catastrophic sensation. A magnetic hook sank into the center of my chest, dragging me toward him with a force that defied gravity. My skin heated, pricking with a desperate, humiliating need to be closer, to touch, to *ground*.

I dug my fingernails into the velvet quilt until the fabric tore.

"Where am I?" My voice was a rusted hinge.

"The Commander's guest suite," Valdus said. He didn't stand. He watched me with eyes that were terrifyingly still. "The Black Hold is too damp. And the guards talk."

"You said I was a prisoner."

"You are." He gestured vaguely to the heavy oak door. "Try the handle."

I didn't move. I knew better than to play his games. "Why am I not in chains, Valdus? Why am I not dead?"

He stood up.

The room shrank. He was a landslide in human form, filling the space with an oppressive, suffocating pressure. He walked toward the bed, his movements fluid and silent.

"Because of the knife you put in my hand," he said softly. He stopped three feet away—close enough for me to smell the sandalwood soap on his skin, far enough that the bond screamed in protest at the distance. "Because now, Vea, we have a problem."

"My name is—"

"I know your name. I know where you sleep. I know you steal bread from the bakers on Fourth Street to feed the orphans in the Warrens." He ticked the items off on his fingers, his face bored. "I know everything."

I stiffened. "Then you know I'm going to kill you."

"You can try."

He reached out. I flinched, expecting a blow. Instead, he picked up a silver tray from the bedside table I hadn't noticed. Roast pheasant. Fresh bread. Wine.

"Eat," he ordered.

"I'm not hungry."

"You are starving. And the bond feeds on calories. If you don't eat, you will pass out, and I will have to force-feed you. Neither of us wants that."

The bond.

I looked at him, really looked at him. The gold in his eyes swirled like molten coins.

"What did you call it?" I asked. "In the office. Carrix."

His expression hardened. The temperature in the room seemed to drop ten degrees.

"Carrix," he repeated. The word sounded like a gavel striking bone. "It is old Fae. Bastardized High Draconic. It means *yoke.*"

He set the tray on the bed.

"It is a biological imperative," he continued, his voice devoid of emotion, as if he were reading a supply report. "Dragon shifters are violent, territorial creatures. To prevent us from slaughtering each other over mates, nature evolved a failsafe. A chemical lock."

He pointed to his chest, then to mine.

"Your blood mixed with mine. The magic recognized a compatible energy signature. It locked us together."

I stared at him. "Compatible? I want to carve your heart out."

"The magic doesn't care about your politics, Little Red. It cares about power. It seeks an equal to balance the scale."

"I am nothing like you."

"No," he agreed, his gaze raking over me with insulting detachment. "You are small. Weak. Fragile. But apparently, your soul is dense enough to anchor mine."

He leaned down, bracing his hands on the mattress on either side of my hips. The scent of him—ozone and heat—flooded my senses. The tether in my chest pulled tight, vibrating with a sickening sort of joy. *Safe. Home. Mine.*

I hated it. I wanted to vomit.

"Here is the reality," Valdus whispered, his face inches from mine. "We are bound. If you die, the feedback loop snaps. My mind breaks. I go feral. I become a true dragon, without the human consciousness to restrain the fire."

He paused, letting the horror of that settle.

"And if I die," he finished, "the fire that now sustains you goes out. You wither. You starve. You die screaming."

He straightened, looming over me like a thunderhead.

"So, you see my dilemma. I cannot kill you. And I cannot let anyone else kill you. Which means you are no longer an assassin. You are an appendage. A liability I must keep breathing to ensure the safety of the Empire."

My hand touched the silver dinner knife on the tray.

It was heavy. Solid. Sharp enough to cut meat. Sharp enough to cut a throat.

"I'd rather die," I whispered.

"Liar."

I moved.

I didn't think; I just let the violence execute the program. I grabbed the knife and launched myself off the bed.

I was fast. I was a blur of motion, driving the blade up toward the soft hollow of his throat.

He didn't dodge. He didn't block.

He caught the blade.

His bare hand wrapped around the silver steel.

"No," he said.

He didn't wince. He didn't bleed.

Heat exploded from his grip.

It wasn't normal heat. It was the concentrated fury of a star. The air warped around his fist. The smell hit me first—acrid and metallic, like pennies left in a furnace.

Then, the silver turned red.

I gasped, releasing the handle as the heat traveled down the metal, searing my fingertips. I scrambled back across the mattress, pressing my spine against the headboard.

Valdus held the knife up. The silver was no longer solid. It drooped like wax, glowing a furious, blinding cherry-red. Droplets of liquid metal hissed as they hit the stone floor, scorching black pits into the rug.

His eyes were fully gold now, the pupils vertical slits. Smoke curled from his nostrils.

He squeezed his fist.

The knife evaporated. It turned into a fine, glittering mist of silver vapor that coated his hand like jewelry.

He opened his palm. Empty.

He looked at me, the dragon retreating behind the man's mask, leaving only the cold, arrogant General.

"Try again, Little Red," he challenged softly. "Find a bigger knife. Find a sword. It won't matter. You cannot cut what burns hotter than the forge."

My chest heaved. My fingers throbbed where the heat had kissed them.

"You're a monster," I breathed.

"I am a weapon," he corrected. "And now, so are you."

He turned and walked to a wardrobe against the far wall. He threw it open and pulled out a bundle of heavy fabric. He tossed it onto the bed. It landed with a thud next to the cooling pheasant.

"Put those on."

I looked at the bundle. Grey wool. Black leather. The insignia of a cadet.

"I'm not joining your army," I spat.

"You can't stay here," Valdus said, fastening a cloak around his shoulders. "The King arrives tomorrow. His sorcerers will smell the bond on you from a mile away. If they find out I'm tethered to a gutter rat, they'll execute us both for treason."

"So what is the plan? You smuggle me out in a laundry cart?"

"No. I hide you in plain sight." He adjusted his gloves, the leather creaking in the silence. "The Storm Citadel houses the War College. New recruits arrive daily. Most die in the first week. No one looks closely at fresh meat."

He turned back to me, his hand resting on the door handle.

"You are now a cadet in the Sky Legion. You will train. You will live in the barracks. You will learn to control that temper."

"And if I refuse?"

"Then I drag you to the cliffs and we see if the bond gives you wings."

I stared at the uniform. It was a death sentence. The War College was a meat grinder. But the alternative was remaining here, in this velvet room, waiting for his King to find me.

Or worse. Waiting for him to come back.

Every minute I spent in his presence, the hook in my chest dug deeper. The bond didn't just want proximity; it wanted submission. It wanted me to crawl to him and beg for the heat of his skin.

I would sooner cut off my own arm.

I stood up, shaking legs finding their strength. I grabbed the uniform.

"Turn around," I growled.

Valdus arched a brow. "I've seen everything there is to see, Vea. You're hardly substantial enough to be modest."

"Turn. Around."

He sighed, a sound of profound irritation, and turned his back.

I stripped off my leathers, my fingers fumbling with the buckles. The air in the room felt charged, pressing against my skin like a physical weight. I pulled on the grey trousers. They were too long. I shoved my arms into the tunic. It swallowed me whole, the shoulders drooping halfway down my biceps.

I looked like a child playing soldier.

I cinched the belt as tight as it would go, but the leather bunched awkwardly.

"Done," I said.

Valdus turned.

His gaze swept over me, starting at my boots and traveling up to the oversized collar that nearly touched my ears. He paused at my waist, where the belt hung loose, then met my eyes.

For a second, the corner of his mouth twitched.

"You look ridiculous," he said flatly.

He opened the door, letting in the roar of the storm and the shouts of drilling soldiers.

"Come on," he ordered, stepping into the hall. "Let's go see how long you survive."

Chapter Five

A Blades Width Apart

The grey wool scratchy against my neck felt less like a uniform and more like a shroud.

I tugged at the collar of the cadet tunic, trying to loosen the chokehold it had on my throat. The fabric smelled of starch and mothballs, a stark contrast to the ozone and blood that clung to the man standing by the balcony doors.

"Stop fidgeting," Valdus said. He didn't turn around. He was staring out at the rain-lashed darkness, his hands clasped behind his back in a pose of military perfection. "You look nervous. Cadets are not nervous. They are eager to die for the glory of the Empire."

"I look like a child playing dress-up," I snapped, tightening the leather belt until it dug into my hipbones. "And I'm not eager to die for your Empire. I'm eager to survive it."

"Then learn to stand still."

He turned. The firelight caught the hard planes of his face, illuminating the exhaustion etched around his eyes. He looked like a statue that had begun to crack under the weight of the sky.

Valdus crossed the room in two strides, invading my personal space with the arrogance of a storm front. He reached out, grabbing the front of my tunic. I stiffened, my hand twitching toward the empty sheath at my hip.

He ignored my flinch. With efficient, impersonal movements, he adjusted the shoulder clasps, pulling the fabric taut so it didn't hang off my frame like a sack. His knuckles brushed my collarbone. The contact sent a jolt of golden heat straight to my core, a sickening, addictive warmth that made my knees weak.

I hated it. I hated that my body recognized him as *safe* when my mind knew he was the executioner.

"Better," he muttered, dropping his hands. "You still look small. But perhaps the drill sergeants will mistake your size for speed."

"I *am* fast."

"You were fast enough to put steel in my hand," he conceded, his gaze dropping to his palm. The wound was gone, healed by his own magic, but the memory of it throbbed between us. "But speed means nothing against dragon fire. Or a gryphon's talons. Or the sort of men who end up at the Storm Citadel."

He walked to the balcony doors and threw them open. The wind howled into the room, extinguishing the candles and sending the tapestries dancing against the stone.

"We leave now," he said. "Before the King's guard secures the perimeter."

I followed him out into the night. The rain had turned to sleet, stinging my cheeks like needles. We were on a private landing platform, a slab of granite jutting out from the Commander's spire with a deadly drop into the churning black water of the moat below.

"Where is the transport?" I shouted over the wind. "Where is the wyvern?"

Valdus began to unbutton his shirt.

My breath hitched. "What are you doing?"

He stripped the black silk from his shoulders, revealing a torso that was a map of violence. Scars crisscrossed his skin—white lines, jagged burns, puncture wounds that had healed badly. He tossed the shirt onto the wet stone. His boots followed. Then his breeches.

I turned my head, staring resolutely at the stone gargoyle on the railing. Heat flushed my neck, warring with the freezing rain.

"Look at me, Vea," he commanded. The voice wasn't human. It was a grind of tectonic plates.

I looked.

He stood naked in the storm, unashamed, a giant of a man carved from shadow and power. But the skin was already rippling. His spine arched, bones cracking with the sound of gunshots.

I stepped back, horror and awe warring in my chest.

His jaw unhinged. His shoulders split. Obsidian scales erupted from his flesh, wet and gleaming like oil. Wings, vast and terrifying, tore from his back, blotting out the lightning. The transformation was brutal, a biological agony that he endured with silent, practiced rage.

In seconds, the man was gone.

In his place crouched a nightmare.

He was massive. A black dragon the size of a warship, his scales absorbing the light rather than reflecting it. Horns curled back from a skull designed for crushing fortifications. His eyes, burning pools of molten gold, fixed on me.

Smoke curled from his nostrils, instantly vaporized by the rain.

Climb.

The word didn't come from his mouth. It exploded in my skull, a telepathic command that vibrated in my teeth.

I stared at the beast. "You want me to... ride you?"

Unless you wish to walk three hundred miles through enemy territory. Climb.

He lowered his left wing, creating a ramp of bone and membrane.

I swallowed the lump of terror in my throat. I had killed men. I had scaled walls. But this? This was madness.

I approached him. The heat radiating from his massive body was intense, a furnace blasting against the sleet. I grabbed a ridge of bone on his wing joint and hauled myself up. The scales were warm and smooth as glass, offering little purchase. I scrambled up his shoulder, finding a hollow between two massive spinal spikes at the base of his neck.

It wasn't a saddle. It was a perilous indent on a living mountain.

Hold the spikes, his voice echoed in my mind, dark and amused. *And do not pull. My scales are sensitive.*

"Shut up," I muttered, wrapping my arms around a spike of black bone that was thicker than my waist.

He didn't warn me.

He launched.

The world dropped away. My stomach remained on the platform. The G-force slammed me against his neck as he drove upward, his wings beating the air with a sound like thunder. We punched through the cloud layer in seconds, leaving the rain behind and entering a realm of silent, freezing moonlight.

The cold hit me instantly. It was a physical blow, stripping the heat from my body. The thin wool of the cadet uniform was useless here, miles above the earth. The air was thin, offering little oxygen.

I gasped, my teeth chattering so hard they ached. Ice crystals formed on my eyelashes.

You are freezing.

"I'm... fine," I lied, burying my face against his warm scales.

You are dying. Humans are so fragile.

The heat beneath me spiked.

It wasn't just his body heat. The bond flared, that golden tether between us pulling taut. Warmth flooded from him into me, not just radiating from his skin, but travelling through the magical connection. It started in my chest and spread to my frozen fingers, a liquid fire that chased away the numbness.

I stopped shivering. I pressed myself closer, my cheek resting against the hard, obsidian armor of his neck. I could hear his heart beating beneath me—a slow, titanic rhythm. *Thrum-thrum. Thrum-thrum.*

It was the most terrifying sound I had ever heard. And the most comforting.

Better?

"Just fly, lizard," I whispered into the wind.

He rumbled, a sound that vibrated through my entire skeleton. We leveled out, soaring north toward the jagged peaks of the Dragontooth Mountains.

For hours, we existed in a void of wind and stars. I should have been plotting my escape. I should have been looking for landmarks. But the bond was a sedative. The rhythmic beat of his wings and the unnatural warmth seeping into my bones lulled me into a trance.

I was riding the monster I had sworn to kill. And God help me, I didn't want to get off.

The sun began to bleed over the horizon, painting the clouds in bruised purples and blood reds, when the destination appeared.

The Storm Citadel.

It wasn't a fortress. It was a wound in the earth.

The War College was built into the vertical face of a mountain that looked like it had been sheared in half by a god's axe. Towers clung to the rock like barnacles, connected by precarious stone bridges that spanned abyssal drops. At the very top, crowned by storm clouds that never dissipated, sat the Citadel itself—a brutalist structure of black iron and grey stone.

Dragons circled the peaks like vultures. Wyverns screeched from lower aeries. The air here was thick with magic, a heavy, metallic taste that coated the back of my throat.

Welcome to hell, Little Red.

Valdus tucked his wings and dove.

We fell out of the sky. The wind screamed past my ears. I buried my face in his neck, screaming silently as the ground rushed up to meet us. At the last possible second, he flared his wings. The air resistance nearly tore me from his back.

We slammed onto a landing pad high up on the mountain, isolated from the main complex. His claws gouged deep furrows into the stone as he skidded to a halt.

I slid off his shoulder, my legs jelly. I hit the ground and stumbled, catching myself on hands and knees. The stone was freezing.

Behind me, the sound of cracking bone returned.

I didn't turn around until the silence settled.

Valdus stood in the center of the landing pad. He was human again. Naked, breathing hard, steam rising from his skin in the frigid morning air. His hair was wild, his eyes still holding a flicker of vertical slit before rounding out to human.

He didn't cover himself. He didn't care. He walked toward me, the predator still very much present in the way he moved.

He stopped, towering over me as I knelt on the stone.

"Rule number one," he rasped, his voice rough from the shift. "You are Cadet Vea. No surname. You are from the borderlands. You have no family."

I stood up, forcing my spine straight. I refused to cower, even though he was a giant and I was... me. "And what happens when someone recognizes the assassin who tried to stick a knife in you?"

"No one saw your face but my guards. And they know better than to speak."

He stepped closer. The heat coming off him was palpable, combatting the mountain chill. He reached out, his thumb tracing the shadow of a bruise under my eye—a bruise I hadn't known was there.

"Rule number two," he said softly. "You do not use your magic. If you feel the shadows rising, if you feel the fire... you find me. Immediately. If the sorcerers detect High Fae markers in your blood, they will dissect you."

"I don't have magic," I insisted, though the memory of the golden light in the office argued otherwise.

"You have *my* magic now," he corrected. "And it is volatile."

He dropped his hand. His gaze hardened.

"Rule number three. This is the most important one."

He leaned down, his face inches from mine. I could see the flecks of obsidian in his golden irises.

"You are mine. The bond makes it so. But here, in this pit of vipers, you are prey. If you let anyone touch you... if you let anyone hurt you..."

He didn't finish the sentence. He didn't have to. The air around us warped, heat shimmering violently.

"I can look after myself, Valdus. I survived the Lower Wards."

"The Wards are a playground compared to this," he said. He straightened, turning to grab a pile of clothes left on a stone bench—spares kept for his arrivals, presumably. He pulled on a pair of black trousers, hiding the magnificent, terrifying reality of his body.

"Get up," he ordered, tossing a cloak at me. "The entrance exams begin in an hour. If you fail, you get sent to the infantry. And the infantry die in the mud."

I caught the cloak. "And if I pass?"

He paused, submitting the buttons of his tunic to his will. He looked at the sprawling, nightmare fortress carved into the cliffside.

"Then you get to die in the sky," he said. "With me."

He walked toward the heavy iron doors leading into the mountain. He didn't look back to see if I was following. He knew I had no choice. The tether in my chest gave a sharp, painful tug, dragging me in his wake.

I looked at the Citadel. It looked like a tomb waiting to be filled.

"Fine," I whispered to the wind. "Let's go to war."

I followed the monster into the dark.

Chapter Six

CLOSE ENOUGH TO BLEED

The training pit smelled of old blood and unwashed bodies.

It was a circular depression carved into the living rock of the mountain, surrounded by steep stone tiers where a hundred other cadets stood jeering. The air was frigid, the wind whipping down from the peaks to bite at exposed skin, but the heat coming off the press of bodies made the atmosphere thick and suffocating.

I stood in the center, the grey wool of my uniform scratching at my neck. It was too big. The sleeves were rolled up three times, and the hem of the tunic hit me at the knees. I looked like a child wearing her father's war gear.

Opposite me stood Varek.

He was a third-year cadet, a slab of beef with eyes like flint and a mouth that hadn't stopped moving since I stepped into the ring. He held a wooden training staff that looked more like a tree trunk in his grip.

"Are they recruiting from the nurseries now?" Varek shouted to the crowd, twirling the heavy staff with insulting ease. "Or did the General mistake the barracks for a kennel?"

Laughter rippled through the tiers. It was a harsh, barking sound.

I didn't laugh. I didn't speak. I shifted my weight, finding purchase on the uneven stone floor. My boots were the only thing that fit me properly—stolen from a dead guard back in the capital, broken in by miles of running.

"Don't worry, Little Red," Varek sneered, stepping closer. "I'll make it quick. Go back to the laundry."

I ignored him. My gaze drifted up.

High above the pit, on an observation balcony protected by an iron rail, stood the High Commander.

General Valdus.

He leaned against the stone balustrade, watching the spectacle with the detached interest of a god observing ants. The distance didn't diminish him. If anything, it made the devastating scale of the man more apparent. He had shed the heavy cloak, standing in a fitted black tunic that did nothing to hide the violence of his build.

The fabric strained across shoulders wide enough to block out the sun. His arms, crossed over his chest, were thick cords of muscle, the sleeves rolled up to reveal forearms roped with veins and scarred skin. My eyes traced the line of his torso, down to where his heavy thighs braced against the stone railing. He was a creature of density and destruction, built to break things. Built to break *me*. The sight of him—that massive, lethal frame held in a deceptively relaxed pose—sent a spike of heat straight to my groin. It was a biological betrayal. My body wanted to climb him like a tree, even as my brain screamed that those hands, currently resting loosely on his biceps, could snap my spine without a tremor of effort.

He was beautiful in the way a forest fire was beautiful. You couldn't look away, even as the smoke choked you.

He caught me looking.

He didn't wave. He didn't smile. He just stared, his golden eyes burning with a cold, terrifying intensity that crossed the distance and slammed into my chest. The bond between us pulled tight, an invisible chain yanking at my navel.

Survive, the look said.

He wouldn't help me. He had brought me here to be forged or broken.

"Eyes on me, rat!"

The air whistled.

instinct took over. I dropped into a crouch a split second before the wooden staff swept through the space where my head had been. The wind of the blow ruffled my hair.

Varek overcommitted to the swing.

I lunged. I didn't have a weapon—cadets earned steel only after surviving the first week—so I used what I had. I drove my shoulder into his solar plexus.

It was like hitting a brick wall.

Varek grunted, stumbling back a step, but he didn't fall. He looked down at me, surprise flaring in his piggish eyes, before the anger took over.

"You little bitch."

He brought the butt of the staff down.

I rolled. Stone bit into my hip. The wood cracked against the floor, sending stone chips flying.

I scrambled to my feet, backing away. He was too big. Too heavy. In the Lower Wards, I would have used a knife. I would have used poison. Here, I had nothing but my hands and the terrifying, volatile magic boiling in my blood.

Don't use it, Valdus had warned. *If you use it, you die.*

I clamped down on the heat rising in my palms.

Varek charged.

This time, I wasn't fast enough.

He feinted left, then swung right. The heavy wood caught me in the ribs.

The impact didn't just hurt; it erased the world.

Air left my lungs in a wet explosion. My vision went white at the edges. I flew sideways, hitting the ground hard enough to rattle my teeth in their sockets. The taste of copper flooded my mouth. I slid across the rough stone, my uniform tearing at the shoulder, skin scraping raw.

"Stay down!" someone shouted from the stands.

I gasped, trying to suck in air that wouldn't come. My ribs felt like they were on fire.

Varek loomed over me, blocking out the grey light of the sky. He placed a heavy boot on my chest and leaned down.

"Pathetic," he spat. Saliva hit my cheek. "The General's new pet breaks easy."

Pressure increased. My sternum creaked.

Panic flared—cold and sharp. Not the panic of losing a fight, but the panic of being crushed.

I looked up. Past Varek's leering face. Past the jeering crowd.

To the balcony.

Valdus hadn't moved. His face was a mask of granite, expressionless. But his hands were no longer crossed. They were gripping the stone railing.

Help me, I didn't say it. I didn't even think it. But the bond screamed it.

A wave of cold rage washed through the tether. It wasn't mine. It was his.

Get. Up.

The command vibrated in my marrow. It wasn't encouragement; it was an order.

Varek pressed harder. "Beg me to stop."

Rage, hot and familiar, eclipsed the pain. I grabbed his ankle.

"Go to hell."

I didn't push him off. I couldn't. He outweighed me by a hundred pounds. instead, I twisted his foot. I dug my nails into the gap between his boot and the greave, finding the sensitive tendon, and I *squeezed*.

Varek howled. His balance wavered.

I moved.

I bucked my hips, throwing him off balance, and scrambled out from under his boot. I didn't stand up. I stayed low, a viper in the dust. Before he could recover, I swept my leg out, catching the back of his knee.

It was a dirty move. A gutter move.

Varek's leg buckled. He went down hard, his heavy armor clattering against the stone.

I didn't wait for him to rise. I was on him. I abandoned the staff, abandoned the rules of honorable combat. I jumped on his back, wrapping my arm around his thick neck.

"Yield!" I screamed, cinching the chokehold tight.

Varek thrashed. He threw himself backward, slamming me into the ground.

My head cracked against the stone. Stars exploded in my vision. The world spun sickeningly. But I didn't let go. I locked my legs around his waist, squeezing the air from his throat.

He clawed at my arm. He punched backward, his fist connecting with my kidney.

Pain blinded me. bile rose in my throat.

Hold, the voice in my head roared. *Hold him.*

I buried my face in his sweaty tunic and squeezed until my muscles burned. Varek's thrashing slowed. His face turned a mottled purple. He gasped, his hands slapping the stone floor.

I released him instantly.

I rolled away, retching dryly, clutching my side. Every breath was a knife in my lungs.

Silence fell over the pit.

The cadets in the stands weren't laughing anymore. They were staring.

I pushed myself up. My legs trembled. Blood dripped from a cut on my forehead, stinging my eye. I wiped it away with the back of my hand, smearing red across my cheek.

Varek lay on the ground, coughing and wheezing, clutching his throat.

I stood over him, swaying slightly.

"I am not a pet," I rasped, my voice raw. "And I don't break."

I looked up at the balcony.

Valdus was looking down. His face was still impassive, but the air around him seemed to shimmer.

His hands were still on the railing.

CRACK.

The sound was like a gunshot in the quiet arena.

Chunks of stone rained down into the pit, dusting the heads of the cadets below.

Valdus had crushed the solid stone balustrade. Powdered granite poured from his fingers like sand. He didn't look at his hand. He didn't look at the damage. He held my gaze for one long, suffocating second.

The message was clear. The stone was a proxy. That was what he wanted to do to Varek. That was what he wanted to do to *anyone* who touched me.

He turned on his heel, his black cape swirling around him, and walked into the shadows of the citadel.

I stood alone in the center of the ring, bleeding and bruised, while the dust of his rage settled around me.

Chapter Seven

TEACHING THE FLAME TO DEVOUR

POV: General Valdus

The rain did not touch me. It fell in sheets, a grey curtain designed to drown the world, but it evaporated an inch from my skin, hissing into steam against the invisible barrier of my heat.

I stood on the iron railing of the observation deck, looking down into the pit.

My beast paced behind my ribs. It scratched at the back of my throat, demanding I jump. Demanding I tear the throat out of the cadet currently swinging a mace at my mate's head.

Mine.

The word was a rhythmic thud in my blood, louder than the storm.

Vea moved through the mud below. She was a blur of motion, small and vicious, a spark trying to survive a tidal wave. She had been in the War College for three days. Three days of bruises. Three days of me watching from the shadows, hands clenched behind my back until the leather of my gloves groaned, forcing myself to do nothing.

If I helped her, they would kill her. If I showed favor, the other cadets would wait until my back was turned and slip a knife between her ribs to test her weakness.

So I let them beat her. I let them drive her into the mud.

And I hated every second of it.

"She is flagging, General."

Lieutenant Kael stood three paces behind me. He was a good soldier. Loyal. He had no idea that the woman down there held the leash to my sanity.

"She is learning," I corrected, my voice a low rumble that vibrated through the iron beneath my boots.

Below, the simulation shifted. This was a night raid drill. No lights. No rules. Just forty cadets in a soup of mud and violence, fighting for a flag that meant nothing.

Vea was cornered. Three second-years had her pinned against the muddy slope of the pit wall. They were big, clumsy boys with too much muscle and not enough discipline. One of them, a lout named Joreen, lunged.

Vea dropped. She didn't absorb the blow; she went under it. She was fast—unnaturally so. But she was exhausted. I could feel her fatigue through the bond. It tasted like ash on my tongue. Her limbs were heavy. Her lungs burned.

The bond between us was a golden wire pulled tight, transmitting her physical state directly into my nervous system. When she took a hit to the shoulder, my own shoulder throbbed. When she gasped for air, oxygen fled the room.

It was torture.

"She's trapped," Kael noted, stepping closer to the rail.

Joreen kicked her.

The blow caught her in the stomach. Vea folded, splashing into the muck.

My hands gripped the railing. The iron heated instantly, glowing a dull, angry cherry-red under my palms.

Get up, Little Red. Get up or I will come down there and kill them, and then I will have to kill everyone who sees it.

She tried to rise. Another cadet slammed a shield into her back, driving her face-first into the slime.

Panic flared in my chest. Not mine. *Hers.*

It wasn't the panic of defeat. It was the panic of loss of control.

The air in the pit changed.

High above, the wind died. The rain stopped falling straight and began to swirl, drawn toward the small, broken figure in the mud.

"General?" Kael's voice held a note of alarm. "The atmospheric pressure..."

I didn't answer. I leaned over the rail, my eyes locking onto her.

Shadows were gathering around her. Not the natural shadows of the night, but something deeper. A void. It leaked from her skin like ink in water, curling around her hands, darker than the storm, darker than death.

She pushed herself up to her knees.

Joreen raised his mace for a finishing blow. "Stay down, rat!"

Vea screamed.

It wasn't a sound of pain. It was a sound of release.

She threw her hands up.

The shadows exploded.

The darkness lashed out physically, a solid wave of kinetic force and cold. It slammed into the three cadets. There was a sickening *crunch* of impact.

Joreen flew backward as if hit by a siege engine. He smashed into the stone wall of the pit twenty feet away and crumpled, sliding down leaving a smear of red on the rock. The other two were thrown into the mud, unconscious before they hit the ground.

Silence slammed into the arena.

Every cadet froze. The instructors on the lower tier stopped shouting.

Vea swayed on her knees. The shadows around her writhed, hungry and confused, before snapping back into her skin.

She looked up. Even from this distance, I saw her eyes. They were pitch black. No whites. No irises. Just the void.

Then, she collapsed.

She fell forward like a puppet with cut strings.

I didn't think. I didn't strategize.

I vaulted the railing.

It was a sixty-foot drop. I didn't slow my descent. I landed in the center of the pit, the impact cracking the stone beneath the mud. A shockwave of dirt and water blasted outward, knocking the nearest cadets off their feet.

"Back!" I roared.

The Voice—the dragon's command—ripped from my throat. It wasn't human. It was a compulsion that slammed into the minds of everyone in the arena.

Cadets scrambled backward, terrified, tripping over themselves to get away from the predator that had just landed in their midst.

I strode to Vea.

She was half-buried in the mud, her face pale as bone, her lips blue. The magic hadn't just protected her; it had eaten her alive. She had no reserves. She was running on fumes, and the explosion had drained her life force to fuel the strike.

I fell to my knees, ignoring the filth ruining my uniform. I gathered her into my arms. She was terrifyingly light. Cold. So cold.

My hand went to her neck. Her pulse was a erratic flutter, a bird dying in a cage.

"No," I snarled. "You do not get to die. I forbid it."

"General Valdus!" An instructor ran forward, sword drawn, confusion marring his face. "Sir, the cadet used unsanctioned magic. Protocol dictates—"

I turned my head.

My eyes were no longer gold. I felt the burn of the vertical slit, the heat of the furnace behind them.

"Protocol," I said, my voice a low, grinding rasp, "dictates that you get out of my way before I melt the flesh from your skull."

The instructor paled. He dropped his sword and scrambled back.

I stood, lifting Vea against my chest. Her head lolled against my shoulder, mud streaking her red hair. The bond screamed in my head—a high, keening wail of *danger, danger, fading, fading.*

I needed to get her to the Spire. I needed to get her out of the wet and the cold.

I marched through the mud, carrying my ruin in my arms.

The cadets parted like the Red Sea. They stared at the unconscious girl, then at me—the High Commander, the Butcher of the Skies—holding her as if she were made of glass.

Let them stare. Let them whisper.

If she died, I would burn them all anyway.

*

I kicked the door to my quarters open.

The fire in the hearth flared as I entered, responding to my agitation. I strode past the war table, past the unread missives from the King, and laid Vea on the heavy teak desk.

I didn't care about the maps. I swept them onto the floor with a crash of inkwells and paper.

"Wake up," I ordered.

She didn't move. She was turning grey. The magic had drained her metabolic energy. It was a parasitic defense mechanism. It had saved her from the mace but was now killing her to pay the debt.

I needed to warm her. I needed to feed the bond so it could feed her.

I ripped my gloves off, throwing them into the corner. My hands were shaking. Not from cold. From terror.

I placed my palms on her cheeks.

"Vea."

Her skin was ice.

I stripped the sodden, muddy tunic from her body. The grey wool tore easily in my grip. I pulled the boots from her feet, the trousers from her legs, until she lay shivering and pale in her smallclothes.

Scars mapped her skin. Silver lines, old burns, the jagged mark on her ribs where a street fight had gone wrong. She was a canvas of violence.

And perfectly, devastatingly beautiful.

I leaned over her, bracing my hands on the desk. I closed my eyes and reached for the fire in my blood. I didn't tamp it down. I didn't leash it. I pulled on the inferno.

Give it to her.

Heat flooded my nervous system. My skin began to glow, a soft, golden radiance that lit the dim room.

I placed my hands on her bare midriff.

The connection was instantaneous.

A jolt of electricity arced between us. The bond snapped taut, a golden highway for the energy I was pouring into her.

She gasped. Her back arched off the desk.

"That's it," I growled. "Take it. take it all."

My magic flowed into her, aggressive and hot. It chased the cold from her veins. Color began to bleed back into her cheeks. Her heart rate steadied, synchronizing with the heavy, thudding rhythm of my own.

Her eyes fluttered open.

They weren't black anymore. They were green. Dazed, pain-clouded, but green.

She looked at me, looming over her, glowing like a forge god.

"Valdus," she whispered. Her voice was a wreck.

"I'm here."

"I... I killed him."

"He's alive," I lied. I didn't know if Joreen was alive. I didn't care. "You need to focus on breathing."

"It hurts." She clawed at her chest. "It feels... empty."

"The magic took everything," I explained, my thumb tracing the line of her hip, pushing heat into the bone. "You overextended. You have Fae markers, Vea. Royal markers. But a human body. It's trying to tear you apart."

She shivered violently. "Cold."

I cursed. My hands weren't enough. The air in the room was too cool, and the desk was sucking the heat from her back.

I scooped her up again.

I carried her to the massive four-poster bed that dominated the far wall. I laid her down on the furs.

"I need to warm you," I said, my voice tight. "Skin to skin. It's the only way to transfer the energy fast enough."

She stared up at me, vulnerability stripped bare. "You're going to...?"

"I am going to save your life," I said roughly. "Do not read anything else into it."

I unbuckled my belt. The heavy leather hit the floor. I stripped off my tunic, then the undershirt. I kicked off my boots.

I hesitated at the trousers.

"Valdus," she murmured. Her eyes drifted shut. "Please."

The plea shattered my restraint.

I stripped the rest off and climbed into the bed.

I was a furnace. A creature of fire. I pulled her small, shivering body against me. Her back pressed into my chest. I wrapped my arms around her, burying my face in the crook of her neck, inhaling the scent of rain and ozone.

The size difference was vivid. A shocking contrast. My arm covered her entire torso. My leg pinned both of hers. She fit against me as if she had been carved from my own rib.

"You're burning," she whispered, relaxing into the heat.

"I am always burning," I muttered against her skin.

It was true. The fire never went out. It only waited.

The bond purred. It felt *right*. It felt inevitable. The magic stabilized, no longer a frantic drain but a steady, rhythmic cycle. My power flowed into her, and her grounding presence calmed the beast in my head.

For the first time in twenty years, the constant, low-level rage in my brain went quiet.

I should have pulled away. She was stable now.

But I couldn't.

Her skin was soft. The curve of her neck was an invitation.

My hand drifted down her stomach, flat and muscled. My thumb brushed the waistband of her smallclothes.

She didn't stop me. She leaned back into me, a small sound of need escaping her throat.

"Valdus," she said again, but this time it wasn't a question. It was a request.

I groaned, a sound torn from the deepest part of my chest.

"You are dangerous, Little Red," I whispered into her hair. "You make me want to burn the world down just to see you smile."

"Then burn it," she breathed.

The permission broke the last chain.

I flipped her over.

She lay beneath me, small and pale against the dark furs, looking up at the monster she was supposed to kill. There was no fear in her eyes. Only a reflection of my own hunger.

I moved down the bed.

"I'm going to heal you," I rasped, my hands parting her thighs. "And then I'm going to make you scream."

I lowered my head.

The beast roared in triumph. The man didn't stand a chance.

*

Chapter 8: The Altar of Bone

The bond was a starving thing.

It didn't want gentle affection. It wanted consumption. It wanted to devour and be devoured.

I knelt between her legs, the heavy velvet of the coverlet bunched beneath my knees. The air in the room was thick, charged with the smell of ozone and sex. The storm outside battered the windows, a pale imitation of the violence rising inside me.

Vea watched me. Her chest heaved, her ribs expanding against pale skin mapped with the history of her pain. She didn't cover herself. She didn't shy away. She looked at me with a terrifying clarity, acknowledging the predator looming over her.

My hands—large enough to crush her skull—rested on her thighs. Her skin was still cool to the touch, but warming under my palms. The contrast made my vision blur. Her fragility was an insult to my nature, and yet, it was the only thing that could anchor me.

"Valdus," she whispered.

My name on her lips was a summon.

I didn't speak. I couldn't. Words were for men, and I was currently very far from being a man.

I ducked my head.

I kissed the soft skin of her inner thigh.

She jerked, a sharp intake of breath hissing through her teeth.

"Easy," I rumbled against her skin. The vibration traveled through her. "I have you."

I moved higher.

The scent of her—aroused, scared, alive—hit me like a drug. It was better than the high of battle. Better than the copper tang of blood.

I found the center of her heat.

She was wet. Slick with desire that betrayed her hatred of me.

I groaned, the sound dragging up from my diaphragm. I licked her.

Vea cried out. Her hips bucked off the mattress. Her hands flew to my hair, fingers tangling in the curls, gripping tight. She wasn't pushing me away; she was holding on for dear life.

"Good girl," I praised, the words rough and unrecognizable. "Feed me."

I didn't give her mercy. I gave her everything else.

I used my tongue, broad and relentless. I tasted the salt and sweet of her. I drank her pleasure like it was the only water in the desert.

Every gasp she made fed the fire in my blood. The golden light under my skin flared brighter, casting long, dancing shadows against the stone walls. The magic flowed from me into her, not through simple touch now, but through this intimate, carnal connection.

I felt her energy spike. The drain from the shadow-burst was refilling, topped off by the sheer intensity of the act.

She tasted like life.

"Valdus... please... too much..."

"Not enough," I growled against her. "Never enough."

I slid two fingers inside her.

She was so tight. So small. My hand looked monstrous against her pale form. I stretched her slowly, fighting the urge to be rough, to claim her with the violence my dragon demanded.

She clamped down around my fingers, a wet, hot fist.

The sensation nearly broke me.

I picked up the pace. My thumb worked the sensitive nub of nerves while my fingers thrust into her, mimicking a rhythm I was desperate to replicate with my body.

Vea's head thrashed against the pillows. "Valdus!"

"I'm here. I'm right here."

She was close. I could feel the tension winding tight in her muscles, the way her breath hitched and caught. The bond between us sang a high, piercing note of anticipation.

"Let go," I commanded. "Give it to me."

She shattered.

It wasn't a gentle release. It was an explosion. She screamed, her back bowing, her fingernails digging into my scalp hard enough to draw blood. Her inner muscles spasmed around my fingers, milking me, pulling at the bond.

Magic—pure, unadulterated power—flooded from her into me.

It hit my brain like lightning.

I saw the universe. I saw the timeline of the world. I saw us, burning together in a pile of ash.

I roared, the sound swallowed by her thighs, as the pleasure-pain feedback loop crested. I didn't climax—I denied myself that release—but the rush of her orgasm through the bond was enough to make my vision go white.

She collapsed back onto the furs, panting, her skin flushed a deep, healthy rose. The grey of death was gone.

I stayed there for a moment, breathing in the scent of her sex and my power. I was shaking.

Slowly, reluctantly, I pulled away.

I crawled up the bed, looming over her.

Vea looked wrecked. Her lips were swollen, her hair a wild halo of fire. She looked at me, eyes wide and green and utterly unguarded.

"You..." she started, then stopped.

I brushed a damp strand of hair from her forehead. My hand was steady now. The rage was gone, replaced by a possessive calm that was infinitely more dangerous.

"You are alive," I said. "That is all that matters."

"You healed me."

"I claimed you."

I lay down beside her, pulling the heavy furs over us. I tucked her against my side, trapping her there. This time, she didn't fight. She curled into me, her hand resting tentatively on the scarred skin of my chest, right over my heart.

"What happens now?" she whispered into the darkness.

I stared at the ceiling, where the shadows still danced, darker than they should be.

"Now," I said, "the world tries to kill us. And we kill it back."

But as I held her, listening to her breathing even out into sleep, the cold fear returned to coil in my gut.

I had felt her power during the climax. It wasn't just shadows. It wasn't just Fae trickery.

It was *Anti-Magic.*

She wasn't just a dragon rider. She was the void that swallowed the light.

The prophecy wasn't a warning. It was a promise.

The Bloodfire Queen will burn the world to ash.

I tightened my arm around her.

Let the world burn. I would be the match.

But I knew, with the terrible certainty of a man watching the sun go down for the last time, that the fire wouldn't start with the enemy.

It would start with us. And when the smoke cleared, only one of us would be left standing in the ruins.

Chapter Eight

Worship in the Wreckage

I lay paralyzed under the sheer, crushing gravity of him.

The storm outside hammered against the glass, a chaotic rhythm that matched the frantic thudding of my heart, but inside the darkened suite, the air was heavy, still, and smelled of ozone and musk. Valdus hovered over me, his massive frame blocking out the firelight, casting me in a shadow that felt safer than it had any right to be.

He was too big. It was a simple, terrifying fact I couldn't reconcile. His shoulders were a wall of muscle and scarred skin, a terrain of violence that stretched wider than the bed should allow. My entire body fit between the span of his knees.

"You are still cold," he murmured. His voice was a low rumble, vibrating through the mattress and into my spine.

"I'm fine," I lied. My teeth wanted to chatter, but I clamped my jaw shut. The magic I had used in the pit had scraped me hollow. It had taken everything—the heat from my blood, the strength from my bones. I was an empty husk, and the void inside me ached with a physical hunger.

"Liar."

Valdus shifted. The movement was predatory, fluid despite his bulk. He settled his weight between my legs, his thighs parting mine with an arrogant ease that made my breath hitch. He didn't ask. He didn't hesitate. He simply took the space because he decided it was his.

His hands, large enough to palm a wyvern's skull, slid up my calves, over my knees, and settled heavy on my thighs. The heat of him seared through my skin. It wasn't just body warmth; it was the furnace of the dragon, the volatile magic that lived in his marrow pushing into mine.

"Valdus," I rasped. "What are you doing?"

"Restoring you," he said, his eyes burning with liquefied gold. "The bond demands equity. You are empty. I am overflowing. I am going to fill you until you scream."

Panic flared—sharp and bright. "I don't need—"

"You need this." His gaze dropped to my stomach, then lower, to the scrap of damp silk I still wore. "And I need to give it."

He gripped the waistband of my smallclothes. The fabric tore. It was a sound like a whispered curse in the quiet room. He tossed the ruined silk aside, leaving me bared to the cool air and his scorching stare.

I should have kicked him. I should have scrambled back against the headboard and reached for the dagger that wasn't there. But the bond... that treacherous, golden tether between us... it didn't want escape. It wanted *this*. It pulled at my navel, dragging me emotionally toward the monster looming over me.

He lowered his head.

My hips bucked instinctively, a useless attempt to retreat. His hands tightened on my thighs, anchoring me to the mattress with the immovability of a mountain range.

"Easy, Little Red," he breathed, his breath hot against the sensory overload of my inner thigh. "I have you."

Then his mouth touched me.

A shockwave rattled my teeth. It wasn't gentle. There was nothing gentle about General Valdus. He licked a stripe of heat up my center, broad and wet and demanding.

I gasped, my head falling back against the velvet pillows. "Valdus!"

He didn't stop. He settled in, his nose brushing against sensitive flesh, inhaling the scent of my arousal. He groaned—a deep, guttural sound of approval that made my toes curl.

"Sweet," he muttered against me. "You taste like ruin."

He used his tongue with devastating proficiency. He found the swollen pearl of nerves hiding in the folds and flicked it, once, twice.

I cried out, my hands flying blindly to his head. My fingers tangled in his thick, dark curls, gripping tight enough to hurt. I wasn't pushing him away. I was holding on for dear life as the floor dropped out from under the world.

The sensation was blinding. Every stroke of his tongue sent a jolt of raw power straight into my core. It wasn't just pleasure; it was life. I could feel the magic pouring from him, a golden river of vitality flooding my depleted veins. The cold that had been eating my bones dissolved, replaced by a feverish, desperate heat.

"That's it," he growled, the vibration against my most sensitive flesh nearly sending me over the edge right then. "Take it. Take everything."

He flattened his tongue, dragging it slow and hard from bottom to top, spreading my own slickness, then sucked hard.

My back arched off the bed. A sob tore from my throat. "Please." I didn't know what I was begging for. For him to stop? For him to never stop?

He ignored the plea, or perhaps he understood it better than I did. He increased the rhythm. His stubble grazed my inner thighs, a rough friction that contrasted maddeningly with the wet heat of his mouth. One of his hands left my leg and slid underneath me, cupping my ass, lifting me to meet his hunger.

He devoured me. He ate like a starving thing, like a dragon finding gold in the mud. There was no hesitation, no awkward fumbling. Just the relentless, punishing attention of a creature who knew exactly how to break me apart and put me back together.

The empty well inside me began to fill. Not with water, but with fire.

Pressure built in my lower belly, a tight, coiling spring of tension that was agonizing and exquisite. The bond sang a high, piercing note in my mind, blurring the line between his pleasure and mine. I could feel his satisfaction, his possessive pride, crashing into my own desperate need.

"Valdus," I choked out, my hips stuttering in his grip. "I can't... it's too much..."

He pulled back for a fraction of a second, his lips slick and swollen. He looked up at me, eyes blown wide, pupils slitted like a beast's.

"Burn for me, Vea," he commanded. "Let go."

He dove back down, sucking harder, his tongue swirling around the peak of my desire.

I shattered.

It hit me like a physical blow. A scream ripped from my lungs, raw and uninhibited. My vision went white. Muscles spasmed, clamping down, milking the sensation as the climax rolled through me in wave after crashing wave.

And with the release came the power.

The magic surged. The connection between us snapped wide open, a floodgate breaking. I felt his strength pouring into me, repairing tissue, fueling blood, knitting the fraying edges of my soul back together.

I thrashed against the mattress, drowning in the feeling of being completely, utterly possessed.

Valdus didn't stop. He drank my release, tasting every tremor, licking the aftershocks until my whimpers turned into ragged, gasping breaths.

Slowly, the world came back into focus.

The ceiling. The dark stone. The firelight dancing on the walls.

And the heavy weight of the man resting his forehead against my thigh.

My chest heaved. Sweat cooled on my skin. I felt... alive. Vibrant. The deadly fatigue from the pit was gone, burned away by the inferno he had just lit inside me.

Valdus lifted his head.

He looked wrecked. His hair was a mess from my fingers, his mouth red and wet with my taste. A dark flush stained his cheekbones. He looked at me with a terrifying intensity, like he was contemplating eating me whole.

He crawled up the bed, the movement slow, stalking.

He braced his arms on either side of my head, caging me in. His chest heaved against mine. I could feel his heart hammering—a slow, titanic rhythm that matched the beat of dragon wings.

"You're back," he stated, his voice a rough scrape against the silence.

I blinked up at him, dazed. "Yes."

He reached out, his thumb tracing the line of my lower lip. His hand was steady, but I could feel the tension vibrating in his frame. He was holding himself back by a thread.

"Good."

He collapsed next to me, rolling onto his back and pulling me into his side. His arm clamped around my waist like an iron band. There was no room for argument. No room for the assassin who hated the general.

There was only the bond, humming with sated contentment.

I rested my cheek on his chest, right over a jagged white scar that looked like a lightning strike. The scent of him—woodsmoke, soap, and sex—filled my nose.

"You saved me," I whispered. The admission tasted like ash.

"I protected my investment," he grunted, staring up at the canopy. But his hand moved on my back, tracing slow, soothing circles that betrayed him.

We lay in silence for a long time, the storm raging outside, impotent against the stone walls.

Finally, I spoke.

"The magic in the pit," I said quietly. "It wasn't fire."

Valdus went still. His hand stopped moving.

"No," he agreed.

"It was dark. It felt... hungry."

He turned his head, looking down at me. The gold in his eyes had cooled, but the danger was still there, sharp as a blade.

"Fire consumes to create heat," he said. "Your magic consumes to create silence. It is the void, Vea. It is the end of things."

A chill that had nothing to do with the temperature swept over me. "The prophecy."

"The Bloodfire Queen," he quoted softly. "She who drinks the light."

He tightened his grip on me, painful and possessive.

"They will come for you," he said. "The King. The Fae. The shadows themselves. They will try to use you or end you."

I looked at the hand resting on my waist—the hand that had just given me pleasure so intense it touched the divine, the hand that had snapped necks and burned cities.

"Let them come," I whispered, surprised by the steel in my own voice.

Valdus smiled. It wasn't a nice smile. It was a baring of teeth, a promise of violence that made the dragon inside him purr.

"Yes," he said, pressing a kiss to the top of my head that felt like a seal. "Let them come. We have plenty of space in the graveyard."

Chapter Nine

The Politics of Possession

Morning didn't break in the Storm Citadel; it bruised.

A sickly, grey light bled through the high arched windows, doing little to combat the shadows clinging to the corners of the room. I woke with a gasp, my lungs seizing as if the air itself had been siphoned away.

Cold.

I was freezing.

The heat that had saturated my marrow the night before was gone, metabolized by a body that was trying to eat itself alive. I curled inward, teeth rattling, seeking the source of the furnace that had kept me tethered to the earth.

Valdus.

He was already awake. He sat on the edge of the mattress, his back to me, a monolith of silence against the storm-battered glass.

I didn't move. I just looked.

He was a creature built for devastation. Without the distraction of his uniform, the unrelenting mass of him was terrifying. Muscles coiled under bronzed skin like steel cables under high tension, shifting with his slightest breath. His back was a map of the Empire's history—a scarred topography of white lash marks, jagged puncture wounds, and the shiny, melted patches of dragon fire burns. He was wide enough to block out the world, dense enough to have his own gravity.

My gaze traveled down the deep groove of his spine to the narrow waist and the heavy, powerful thighs that had pinned me to this bed only hours ago.

A want, sharp and humiliating, spiked in my belly.

It wasn't affection. It was addiction. It was the biological trap sprung by the bond, demanding I crawl onto his lap and beg for the friction of his skin.

"Stop staring," he rumbled.

He didn't turn around. He reached for a glass of water on the nightstand, the crystal looking fragile and ridiculous in his grip.

"I'm cold," I admitted, my voice scraping like sandpaper.

He froze. The glass cracked in his hand.

Water dripped onto the stone floor. Valdus ignored it. He turned slowly, the movement predatory and smooth. His eyes were molten gold, the vertical pupils blown wide.

"I can feel it," he said. "The drain. Your body is a sieve, Vea."

He stood up and loomed over the bed. The sight of him—fully nude, visibly aroused, and looking at me like I was a meal—made my heart hammer against my ribs.

"We have an audience with the Court Sorcerers in an hour," I said, pulling the fur blanket up to my chin. "I need clothes. I need a weapon."

"You need fuel."

He ripped the furs from my grip.

The cold air hit my skin like a slap. I flinched, curling into a ball, but he was there instantly. He climbed over me, his weight settling around my hips, caging me in. He didn't offer comfort. He offered survival wrapped in depravity.

"Spread your legs," he ordered.

"Valdus, the guards will be—"

"The guards know better than to enter a dragon's den when the door is barred." He grabbed my ankles and pulled. I slid down the mattress, completely exposed to his gaze. "You are grey, Little Red. If you walk into that council room like this, Malgor will smell the weakness on you and strip the flesh from your bones."

He didn't wait for permission. The bond didn't require it. The golden tether between us snapped taut, vibrating with his intent.

He lowered his head.

His mouth covered me.

I arched off the bed, a scream dying in my throat as the connection slammed into place. It wasn't gentle. It was a transfusion. His tongue was hot, wet velvet, working with a relentless, punishing rhythm that had nothing to do with romance and everything to do with possession.

Magic flooded my system.

It roared through my veins, chasing away the frost, sparking fires in my fingertips. I tangled my hands in his thick, dark curls, pulling him closer, anchoring myself against the onslaught.

"Good girl," he growled against me, the vibration sending shockwaves through my pelvis. "Take it."

He drank from me as if I were a chalice, his hands gripping my thighs hard enough to bruise. He found the center of my nerves and didn't let up. He bullied the pleasure out of me, demanding a response, demanding the surrender that my mind refused to give but my body couldn't withhold.

The world narrowed to the wet heat of his mouth and the heavy weight of his hands. The ceiling spun. The grey light turned to gold.

I shattered.

The climax ripped through me, violent and absolute. I sobbed his name, my hips bucking against his face, the magic transfer peaking in a blinding flash of white heat.

Valdus drank every drop of it. He rode out the tremors with me, his breathing harsh and ragged against my skin.

Then, silence.

He pulled back. He rested his forehead against my thigh for a heartbeat, composing the monster, before lifting his head. His mouth was slick, his eyes burning with a satisfaction that terrified me.

"Better," he stated.

He rolled off the bed and strode toward the wardrobe as if he hadn't just had his face between my legs. The shift was jarring. One second he was a lover; the next, he was the High Commander, cold and distant as the peaks outside.

The loss of his contact was a physical blow. The warmth remained in my blood, but the skin-hunger ached, a phantom limb syndrome that left me hollow.

He tossed a bundle of clothes at me.

"Get dressed," he said, his back to me as he pulled on his breeches. "The vultures are waiting."

*

The corridor leading to the Council Chamber was a gauntlet of stone and malice.

Every step echoed. The walls were lined with tapestries depicting the burning of the rebellion—my people, turned to ash by the man walking a step ahead of me.

Valdus wore his formal blacks. The high collar hid the pulse point of his throat; the silver epaulets gleamed like knives. He didn't look at me. He walked with a lethal grace, one hand resting on the pommel of his sword, the other swinging loose.

I struggled to keep up, my shorter stride forcing me into a near-trot. The uniform he had given me was better fitted than the cadet wool—black leather, reinforced at the ribs, with a hidden sheath for the dagger I had stolen from his desk.

"Stay behind me," Valdus murmured as the iron doors loomed ahead. "Do not speak unless addressed. And for the love of the gods, do not bleed on anything."

"I'm not the one who usually does the bleeding," I muttered.

"Today, you are."

The doors groaned open.

The Council Chamber was a cavernous rotunda built over the open mouth of the mountain. Wind whistled up through the floor grates. At the center stood a obsidian table, and around it, the architects of the Empire's misery.

Three men. Two women.

And Malgor.

The High Sorcerer stood at the head of the table. He was a withered thing, his skin the color of parchment, draped in robes of iridescent beetle-green. But it wasn't his appearance that made my stomach turn.

It was the smell.

He smelled of sulfur and old graves. As we entered, the air in the room seemed to curdle, heavy and thick with a magic that tasted like copper on the back of my tongue.

Malgor turned. His eyes were milky white, blind to the light but seeing everything else.

"General," Malgor rasped. His voice sounded like dry leaves skittering on stone. "And the... acquisition."

Valdus stopped ten feet from the table. I halted in his shadow, my hand hovering near my hip.

"She is a cadet," Valdus corrected, his voice bored. "Cadet Vea. You requested her presence for the intake assessment."

"We requested the girl who put a knife in your hand," a woman to the left said. She was beautiful and sharp, like a diamond waiting to cut. "We hear she has spirit."

"She has luck," Valdus said. "And poor aim."

Malgor stepped forward. He didn't walk; he glided, the hem of his robes hovering an inch above the floor. He stopped in front of Valdus, then leaned around the General's massive bulk to peer at me.

Those dead white eyes fixed on my face.

"She smells," Malgor whispered. He inhaled deeply, a rattling sound. "She smells of... ozone. And smoke. And *you*, General."

My blood went cold.

Valdus didn't finch. "She rides my dragon. The scent carries."

"Does it?" Malgor smiled. His teeth were filed to points. "Or is it something deeper? The bond creates... appetites."

"Test her," Valdus ordered, stepping sideways to block Malgor's view of me. The movement was subtle, but it was a wall slamming down. "Or are we done here?"

Malgor gestured with a skeletal hand. A silver bowl sat on a pedestal nearby.

"The blood," the Sorcerer commanded.

I looked at Valdus. His jaw was set in granite. *Do it,* the bond whispered. *I am right here.*

I stepped forward. I drew the dagger from my boot—not the one Valdus gave me, but my own rusted iron blade. I sliced my palm.

Blood welled, thick and dark. I held my hand over the bowl. It dripped. *Plink. Plink. Plink.*

The liquid hit the silver and hissed.

Smoke rose from the bowl. Not grey smoke. purple smoke.

The room went silent.

The purple mist swirled, forming shapes—crowns, thorns, broken chains.

Malgor's head snapped up.

"Royal markers," he hissed. "High Fae."

The woman at the table stood up, her chair scraping loudly. "Impossible. The royal lines were extinguished."

"Not all of them," Malgor whispered. He looked at me with a sudden, terrifying hunger. "A halfling. Hidden in the gutter. A mongrel bitch with the blood of queens."

He raised his hand. Green fire ignited at his fingertips.

"Seize her," Malgor screeched. "She is an abomination! We must dissect the source!"

Guards stepped out from the shadows, spears lowered.

I crouched, adrenaline flooding my system.

"Touch her," Valdus said softly, "and you die."

"This is treason, Valdus!" Malgor shouted. The green fire flared, casting sick shadows on the walls. "She is a threat to the King! Stand aside!"

Malgor threw the fire.

It wasn't aimed at me. It was aimed at Valdus, a distraction to get to the prize behind him.

Valdus didn't draw his sword. He didn't shift.

He simply moved.

He caught the bolt of green fire in his gloved hand. He crushed it. The magic fizzled out with a pathetic whine.

Then he lunged.

It was too fast to track. One second he was standing there; the next, he had crossed the distance to Malgor.

His hand—the one that had just given me paradise—wrapped around the Sorcerer's throat.

He lifted Malgor off the floor. The old man kicked, his robes flapping.

"You forget your place, wizard," Valdus snarled. The air in the room heated instantly. The tapestries began to smoke. "I command the Sky Legion. I command the dragons. And I decide who is a threat."

"The King..." Malgor choked out, clawing at Valdus's wrist.

"The King is three hundred miles away," Valdus said. "And you are here. Alone. With a monster."

Valdus squeezed.

There was a wet, sickening crunch.

Malgor went limp.

Valdus dropped the body. It hit the floor with a heavy thud, the head lolling at an unnatural angle.

Silence stretched tight enough to snap.

Valdus turned to the table. His eyes were burning gold trenches into the remaining council members. He pulled a handkerchief from his pocket and wiped his glove, though there was no blood.

"The test was inconclusive," Valdus said flatly. "The machinery malfunctioned. The Sorcerer was incompetent."

He looked at the woman who had stood up.

"Is there a disagreement?"

The woman looked at the dead body of the High Sorcerer, then at the dragon in human skin standing over it. She slowly sat back down.

"None, General," she whispered. "A tragic accident."

"Good."

Valdus turned to me. He extended a hand. It was steady. Large. Capable of ending worlds or saving them.

"Come, Cadet," he said. "We have training to do."

I looked at the corpse. I looked at the man who had killed for me without a second of hesitation.

I took his hand.

His fingers closed over mine, warm and calloused and terrifyingly safe.

We walked out of the chamber, leaving the smell of death behind us, stepping into a war that had just become personal.

Chapter Ten

RIDING THE RUIN

The iron door to the aerie slammed shut behind us, sealing away the stench of the dead sorcerer, but the smell of ozone and burnt magic clung to Valdus like a second skin.

He didn't stop. He didn't speak. He towed me through the cavernous stone hangar, past the empty stalls where other riders kept their wyverns, toward the massive archway that opened onto the nothingness of the sky. The wind up here was a physical assault, a screaming gale that tore at my hair and stung my eyes, but Valdus walked into it as if it were a gentle breeze.

He released my hand only when we reached the edge of the precipice. A thousand feet below, the jagged teeth of the mountain range waited to swallow the careless.

Valdus turned to me. The gold in his eyes was spinning, turbulent and bright. He looked less like a man and more like a reactor shielding a meltdown. The killing in the council chamber hadn't sated him; it had only woken the beast fully.

"Strip," he ordered. The word was swallowed by the wind, but the command vibrated in my skull.

I stared at him. "Here? Now?"

"Your clothes are not rated for altitude," he shouted over the gale. "And they will burn when I turn. The heat transfer is... significant."

He didn't wait for me to argue. He began to unfasten his own tunic. The black military jacket hit the stone floor, followed by the shirt, boots, and breeches. He stood nude against the backdrop of the storm-grey sky, a monument of scarred muscle and violence. The cold should have shriveled him. Instead, steam rose from his shoulders.

I fumbled with the laces of my leather gear, my fingers numb. I stripped down to the smallclothes Valdus had ruined earlier and the tunic I wore beneath the armor.

"Valdus," I called out, my voice thin against the wind. "What are we doing?"

"Malgor was a symptom," he said, his voice dropping into a register that rattled my teeth. "The disease is everywhere. If you are going to survive the rot in this kingdom, you cannot just be a rider. You must be part of the sky."

He stepped toward the ledge.

"Watch."

He didn't jump. He fell forward.

For a heartbeat, he was just a man falling to his death.

Then, the sound hit me.

It wasn't a magical shimmer. It was the wet, sickening crunch of anatomy rewriting itself. Bones snapped and lengthened with the crack of rifle fire. Skin split, giving way to an eruption of obsidian scales that absorbed the light. A roar shattered the air, loud enough to stop my heart, as wings the size of mainsails exploded outward, catching the updraft.

The man was gone.

In his place hovered a nightmare.

He was massive. A creature of midnight and malice, easily fifty feet from snout to tail. His scales were armor plates of black glass, scarred from centuries of war. Horns crowned his head like a jagged coronet, and his eyes—huge, burning orbs of molten gold—fixed on me with an intelligence that was both terrifying and familiar.

Smoke vented from nostrils that glowed like volcanic fissures.

The dragon hovered level with the ledge, the wind from his wingbeats nearly knocking me off my feet. He turned his massive head, offering his neck.

Climb.

The voice wasn't spoken. It slammed into my mind, heavy and ancient. It wasn't the Valdus who spoke in the strategy room. This voice tasted of ash and iron.

I hesitated. My survival instincts, honed in the gutters where rats ate the weak, screamed at me to back away. To hide.

But the bond in my chest pulled tight. It was a hook in my navel, dragging me toward the ledge. The heat radiating from him was a siren call in the freezing air.

I stepped onto the ledge. I reached out.

My hand touched the warm, slick scales of his neck.

Do not fall, the voice rumbled in my head. *I will catch you, but the drop will be unpleasant.*

I grabbed a ridge of bone near his spine and hauled myself up. The heat was immense. It soaked through my thin tunic, searing my thighs. I settled into the hollow between his shoulders, where the scales formed a natural saddle, rough and warm.

"Don't drop me," I muttered, gripping a spine of bone until my knuckles turned white.

Valdus didn't answer. He simply stopped hovering.

He tucked his wings.

We dropped.

My stomach left my body. The air rushed out of my lungs in a strangled gasp. The stone wall of the Citadel blurred into a grey streak as we plummeted toward the jagged rocks below. Gravity clawed at me, trying to rip me from his back.

Just before we hit the spikes, his wings snapped open.

The sound was like thunder cracking inside a canyon. The membrane caught the air, and the sudden deceleration slammed me against his neck.

We didn't glide. We didn't dance. We tore through the clouds.

Valdus climbed with a violence that defied physics. He carved a path through the sky, banking hard enough that the horizon tilted ninety degrees. The wind roared, a deafening continuous explosion, but in the lee of his neck, the air was hot and breathable.

Open your mind, Little Red.

The command filtered through the terror.

Blocking me out is dangerous. We must sync.

I didn't know how to open my mind. I only knew how to build walls. I had spent my life hiding—hiding my location, hiding my food, hiding my fear.

Let the walls down, he urged. His presence pressed against my mental barriers like a physical weight. *Let me in.*

I closed my eyes against the stinging wind and focused on the golden tether between us. I stopped fighting the pull.

The barrier shattered.

His mind flooded mine.

It wasn't thoughts. It was sensation.

Rage.

A vast, oceanic rage that had been burning for decades. It was the fury of a creature bred for war, chained by duty to a kingdom he despised. I felt the constant, grinding pressure of his restraint—the effort it took him not to burn the Citadel to the ground every single day. I felt his isolation, a cold, dark void that no amount of power could fill.

And beneath the rage, beneath the ice... I felt me.

His awareness of me was hyper-focused. He felt the grip of my thighs on his scales. He felt the frantic beat of my heart against his spine. He felt a fierce, terrifying possessiveness that eclipsed everything else. To him, I wasn't just a rider. I was the only thing in the world that mattered. Everyone else was kindling.

I feel you, I projected back, clumsy and raw.

Good.

The sensation of approval was like a warm hand on the back of my neck.

Now feel the sky.

He banked left, diving through a bank of clouds. Moisture slicked my skin, then evaporated instantly against his heat.

He showed me the currents. I didn't see them; I felt them through him. The air was a landscape of pressure ridges and thermal columns. I felt the drag on his left wing, the lift under his tail.

Lean, he instructed.

I leaned left.

He responded instantly, sharpening the turn, diving faster.

We weren't two beings anymore. We were one entity of claw and scale and terrified human heart. The exhilaration was a drug. The fear evaporated, replaced by a sense of power so absolute it was intoxicating. I was flying. I was the apex predator. The world below was small, insignificant. The people who had hurt me, the guards who had beaten me, the hunger that had defined me—they were nothing from this height.

We carved through the atmosphere, climbing higher until the air grew thin and the sky turned a bruised purple.

Valdus leveled out. We drifted on a high thermal, the only sound the rhythmic *whoosh* of his wings and the thundering of my own pulse.

Below us, the world was a map of snow and stone.

This is what you are fighting for, his voice rumbled, softer now. *Not the King. Not the content of the maps. This.*

"Freedom," I whispered, though I knew he caught the thought.

Control, he corrected. *The only freedom is the power to say no.*

He tipped his wings, beginning a long, spiraling descent toward a jagged peak that pierced the cloud layer like a spear. It was a desolate spire of black rock, flat at the top, covered in ice that gleamed like diamonds.

He landed with a heavy impact that shook the mountain. talons gouged deep furrows in the stone as he skidded to a halt, wings flared to bleed off speed.

Steam hissed as he settled onto the ice.

I slid down his flank, my legs wobbling as my boots hit the frozen ground. The cold rushed in instantly, biting at my exposed skin, but the residual heat coming off him kept the worst of it at bay.

I turned to look at him.

He was already shifting.

The process was just as violent in reverse. Scales receded, bones cracked and compressed. The massive bulk of the dragon collapsed inward, reforming into the severe, ruthless lines of the General.

He stood on the ice, naked and steaming, his chest heaving. His skin was flushed, the scars standing out in stark white relief against the bronze. He looked wild. The civilized mask he wore at court was gone, burned away by the flight.

He walked toward me. The ice didn't seem to bother him. He was the fire.

"You didn't fall," he said. His voice was rough, wrecked by the transition.

"I held on," I managed. My own voice was shaky. "You run hot."

"I am a furnace," he agreed. "And you were freezing."

He stopped inches from me. He towered over me, blocking the wind. His golden eyes searched my face, looking for fear, looking for rejection.

"Why did you bring me here?" I asked.

"Because down there," he gestured vaguely toward the cloud layer hiding the world, "there are ears in the walls. Shadows that listen. Here, there is only the wind."

He reached out. His hand, hot and heavy, cupped my jaw. His thumb brushed my cheekbone, smearing a droplet of cloud-moisture.

"You killed Malgor," I said. It wasn't a question.

"I removed an obstacle."

"He was a High Sorcerer. The political fallout..."

"Let the politicians choke on it," Valdus snarled softly. His fingers tightened on my jaw. "He looked at you as if you were a specimen. He wanted to cut you open."

The rage I had felt in the bond flared again, hot and suffocating.

"I could have handled him," I lied.

"No, Vea. You couldn't." He leaned down, his forehead resting against mine. The contact sent a jolt of electricity straight to my toes. "You are lethal, Little Red. I know that. But you are playing a game where the rules are written in blood you don't have yet. Malgor would have flayed your mind before you could draw your dagger."

"So you protect me?" I challenged, staring into his burning eyes. "Is that it? The big dragon protects his hoard?"

"Yes." The admission was blunt. "You are mine. The bond makes it so. The prophecy makes it so. I will burn the entire Council to ash before I let them touch you."

"And what if I burn the world?" I whispered. "That's what the book said. The Bloodfire Queen."

Valdus pulled back slightly to look at me. His expression was unreadable, hard and beautiful in the harsh light.

"Then we burn it together," he said. "The world is broken anyway. Maybe it needs a fire."

He looked at my mouth.

The air between us charged, crackling with static. My breath hitched. The cold, the danger, the murder—it all faded into the background, leaving only the gravitational pull of him. I wanted to close the gap. I wanted to taste the violence on his lips.

My hands flattened against his bare chest, feeling the heavy, slow beat of his heart.

"Valdus," I breathed.

He started to lower his head. His eyes drifted shut, his lashes dark against his cheek.

SCREEE!

The sound cut through the air like a knife.

Valdus froze. His eyes snapped open, the gold instantly hardening into steel.

He spun around, placing himself between me and the sky.

A hawk, black-feathered and streaked with silver, dove from the clouds. It wasn't a natural bird. Its eyes glowed with blue magelight, and metal talons glinted in the sun. It carried a scroll case banded in crimson iron.

A war messenger.

The bird shrieked again, circling before landing on a jagged outcropping of rock. It extended its leg.

Valdus cursed, a foul, guttural sound.

"Don't touch it," he ordered.

He strode to the bird. He didn't offer a treat; he snatched the scroll case from its leg with a roughness that made the construct snap its beak at him. He broke the seal with his thumb.

He unrolled the parchment.

I watched his back. The muscles tensed, shifting under the skin like coiling snakes. The silence on the peak grew heavy, the earlier intimacy shattering under the weight of reality.

"What is it?" I asked, stepping closer. "The Council?"

"No."

Valdus crushed the parchment in his fist. Paper turned to ash in his grip, smoke curling between his fingers.

He turned to face me. The lover was gone. The General was back.

"Get on my back," he commanded, his voice devoid of warmth. "We leave now."

"Valdus?"

"The Northern Border," he said, his eyes scanning the horizon as if he could see the enemy from here. "The Fae have breached the Rift. They aren't just raiding, Vea. They've brought siege beasts."

He looked at me, and for the first time, I saw a flicker of true fear in those golden depths. Not for himself. For me.

"They are hunting," he said grimly. "And they are asking for you by name."

He stepped back, his form already blurring, bones cracking as the dragon rushed to the surface.

Climb, Little Red, his voice boomed in my head, urgent and terrified. *We are going to war.*

Chapter Eleven

A Massacre in Her Name

I drove my wings downward, catching the thin, freezing air of the upper atmosphere.

The impact of the message scroll still burned in my mind, hot as a branding iron. *Siege beasts. The Rift.*

It wasn't a skirmish. It was an extinction event.

Beneath me, the granite spine of the Dragon's Tooth rushed up to meet us. I didn't slow down. I couldn't. Every second spent in the air was a second the enemy moved closer to the Citadel walls—closer to *her*.

I felt Vea's terror through the bond. It wasn't for herself. It was the primal, lizard-brain fear of the fall. She clung to the ridges of my neck, her small body pressed so tight against my scales she felt like a second skin. Her heartbeat hammered against my spine, a frantic drumbeat that synced with the rage boiling in my blood.

Hold on, I commanded, the Voice booming through our shared mental space.

I flared my wings at the last possible second. The membrane snapped taut with a sound like a thunderclap. Air displaced with enough force to strip the snow from the peaks.

I hit the landing platform of the Storm Citadel.

Stone cracked. The entire tower shuddered under the weight of fifty tons of apex predator. I dug my talons deep into the rock, carving furrows of spark and dust as I skidded to a halt, putting my body between the open sky and the rider on my back.

Get down.

Vea scrambled off my shoulder, sliding down the slope of my wing to the flagstones.

I didn't wait. I let the magic go.

The shift was agony. It always was. It felt like being broken on a wheel and put back together by a madman. Bones snapped, compressed, and restructured. Scales receded, burning as they dissolved into human skin. The massive, furnace-heat of the dragon collapsed into the dense, compact form of the man.

I hit my knees, gasping, steam rising from my naked shoulders in the biting wind.

Pain was old news. I ignored it. I looked up.

Vea stood three feet away.

She was shaking. Her lips were a dangerous shade of violet, her skin pale as milk against the dark leather of her gear. The flight had frozen her.

I stood, the cold air meaning nothing to the fire still churning in my veins.

The contrast between us sickened me. I was indestructible. I could fly through a volcano; I could sleep in a glacier. But she... she was so fragile. A hollow-boned thing that could be snapped by a stiff wind or a careless hand.

And yet, she was the anchor holding me to the earth.

I crossed the distance in a single stride. I grabbed her arms, my hands covering her biceps entirely.

"You're freezing," I snarled, pulling her against my chest. I flooded the bond with heat, pushing my own metabolic fire into her.

"I'm fine," she chattered, her teeth clicking together. She didn't pull away. She leaned into me, stealing my warmth. "The scroll... Valdus, what did it say?"

"Later."

"Now." She grabbed my forearms, her fingers digging in. "If we are going to die, I want to know what kills us."

I looked down at her. The wind whipped her red hair across her face, masking the scar on her cheek. She didn't look like a victim. She looked like a blade that had just been sharpened.

"The Fae haven't just crossed the border," I said, my voice low and dangerous. "They brought the Hollow."

Vea went still. "The stories? The living darkness?"

"It's not a story. It's a plague. A magical cancer that eats the land, the air, and the light." I gripped her tighter, needing to feel the solidity of her form to confirm she hadn't dissolved yet. "It doesn't just kill, Vea. It unmakes. And they are marching it straight for the Citadel."

The heavy oak doors to the aerie burst open.

Kael sprinted onto the landing deck, his sword drawn, flanked by four of my personal guard. He skidded to a stop when he saw me—naked, steaming, and clutching the new cadet like she was the last scrap of food in a famine.

He didn't blink. He holstered his blade and threw me a cloak.

"General," Kael barked. "The War Council is assembled. General Jarek is demanding command of the Sky Legion."

I caught the heavy fur cloak and swung it around my shoulders, wrapping Vea inside it with me in one fluid motion.

"Jarek," I spat the name like a curse. "He couldn't command a dog to sit, let alone a dragon to kill."

"He says you're compromised," Kael said, his eyes flicking briefly to Vea. "He says the bond has made you... unstable."

I laughed. It wasn't a nice sound. A gout of black smoke escaped my lips with the exhale.

"Unstable?" I started walking, dragging Vea with me, keeping her tucked against my side under the cloak. "I'll show him unstable."

We moved through the stone corridors of the Citadel. The atmosphere had shifted. Gone was the rigid order of the military academy. In its place was the frantic, hushed panic of a city under siege. Servants ran with armfuls of supplies. Cadets huddled in alcoves, whispering, their faces pale.

They smelled of fear.

Sour sweat. Urine. Desperation.

It grated on my senses. My dragon wanted to roar, to dominate the space and silence the noise. I clamped down on the urge.

Vea matched my pace, though she had to jog to keep up with my stride. She didn't ask where we were going. She knew.

We reached the heavy iron doors of the War Room. Two guards crossed their pikes to bar the way.

"General," one stammered. "General Jarek ordered—"

"Move," I said.

I didn't raise my voice. I didn't draw a weapon. I simply let the vertical slits of my pupils bleed into my vision and pushed a fraction of the dread I carried outward.

The guards blanched. They scrambled back, pikes clattering against the stone.

I kicked the doors open.

The War Room was a cavern of maps and shouting. A dozen commanders stood around the central table, arguing over logistics.

General Jarek stood at the head. He was a thick-necked man who had earned his rank through politics rather than blood. He looked up as the doors slammed against the walls.

Silence fell.

Jarek's eyes narrowed. "Valdus. You're late. And you're out of uniform."

"I was busy," I said, walking to the table. The other commanders parted like water, giving me a wide berth. I didn't let go of Vea. I kept her tucked into my side, my arm a heavy weight around her waist.

"Busy playing nursemaid to a gutter rat?" Jarek sneered, gesturing to Vea. "While the Northern Border burns?"

Vea stiffened against me. I squeezed her hip—a warning wait.

"The border isn't burning, Jarek," I said, leaning over the map. "It's rotting. There's a difference."

I reached out and swept his markers off the parchment.

"Hey!" Jarek lunged forward.

I caught his wrist. I didn't squeeze hard—just enough to grind the bones together. He gasped, his face turning red.

"Sit down," I ordered. "Before I decide I don't need a co-commander."

I shoved him back. He stumbled into his chair.

I pointed to the map, tracing the line of the Rift. "The message wasn't just a declaration of war. It was a scouting report."

"We know," Kael said, stepping up to the table. "Our sorcerers felt the shift. The magical pressure is enormous. It's not just troops, sir. It's... something else."

"The Void," I said. "They are using the Hollow to pave the road. It eats magic. It eats life. If we send the infantry into that, they won't die fighting. They'll just cease to exist."

A murmur of horror went through the room.

"Then we use the dragons," Jarek said, rubbing his wrist. "Burn it out."

"Fire feeds it," Vea said.

Her voice was quiet, but it cut through the room like a razor.

Jarek looked at her, his lip curling. "Speak when spoken to, cadet. You have no standing here."

"She has more standing than you," I rumbled, the golden light in my eyes flaring. "She has faced the void. In the pit. Yesterday."

Jarek laughed. "Accidental magic from a untrained mongrel. And now you bring her here? To a strategy meeting? She is a security risk, Valdus. She tried to kill you three days ago."

"And she failed," I said flatly. "Lucky for the Empire."

"Is it?" Jarek stood up, leaning his knuckles on the table. "The enemy isn't just marching blindly, Valdus. We intercepted a courier an hour ago. They have demands."

My blood ran cold. The beast in my chest uncoiled, hissing.

"What demands?"

Jarek smiled. It was the smile of a man who thought he held a winning hand.

"They want the girl."

The air in the room vanished.

Vea went rigid.

"They call her the Ember," Jarek continued, watching my face closely. "Or the Spark. They say she belongs to the Shadow King. Hand her over, and they will halt the advance for a month. Enough time to evacuate the outer provinces."

He straightened his tunic. "It's a strategic exchange, High Commander. One life. A criminal's life, at that. For thousands."

Red haze clouded my vision.

The furniture in the room began to rattle. The torches on the walls flared, turning from orange to blinding white.

"No," I said.

The word was quiet. But the stone floor beneath my boots cracked.

"Be reasonable," Jarek argued, looking around the room for support. "She is a liability. The prophecy—"

"I don't care about the prophecy," I roared.

The sound hit them like a physical blow. Glass shattered in the window frames. Commanders ducked, covering their heads.

I released Vea and stalked toward Jarek.

He backed up, tripping over his chair. "Valdus—"

I grabbed him by the throat. I lifted him off the ground, pinning him against the stone wall. My skin was burning, the heat radiating off me enough to singe the fabric of his uniform.

"Listen to me closely," I snarled, my face inches from his. "Because I will only say this once."

I tightened my grip. His eyes bulged.

"She is not a bargaining chip. She is not a sacrifice. She is *mine*."

The word echoed in the silence. It wasn't a romantic declaration. It was a territorial claim. It was the dragon stating ownership of the hoard.

"If you suggest handing her over again," I whispered, the smoke curling from my mouth, "I will peel the skin from your body and fly your flayed corpse over the enemy lines as a warning. Do you understand?"

Jarek nodded frantically, clawing at my hand.

I dropped him.

He collapsed, wheezing, clutching his throat.

I turned back to the room. The other commanders were staring at me with wide, terrified eyes.

"The girl stays," I said, adjusting my cloak. "We fight. We hold the line at the Storm Citadel. If the Void wants to eat, it can choke on dragon fire."

"Sir," Kael stepped forward, his voice steady despite the tension. "If they are targeting her... keeping her here is dangerous. For her. And for the Citadel. If she falls into their hands..."

"I know," I said.

I looked at Vea.

She was standing by the table, her hand resting on the hilt of the dagger I had given her. She wasn't looking at Jarek. She was looking at me.

Her eyes were green fire. There was no gratitude in them. Only a hard, glittering resolve.

"I'm not going to hide in the cellar, Valdus," she said.

My jaw tightened. "You are not ready for this. You can barely control your own magic."

"Then teach me," she challenged. "Or get out of my way."

"You will die."

"Then I die on my feet," she stepped closer, right into my personal space. The size difference was laughable—she had to crane her neck to look me in the eye—but her presence was massive. "I spent my whole life in the gutters, running from men like Jarek. Running from men like *you*. I am done running."

She poked a finger into my chest, right over my heart.

"You claimed me, General. You said I was yours. Well, if I'm yours, then you don't get to trade me for safety. You use me to win."

The audacity. It hit me like a shot of whiskey.

My dragon roared in approval. *She has teeth,* he purred. *She bites.*

I looked at the map. The encroaching darkness. The sheer impossibility of the odds.

Then I looked back at the tiny, furious woman who held the leash to my sanity.

"Fine," I growled.

I grabbed a piece of charcoal and marked a location on the map—the Eastern Battlement.

"You are mobilized. You will be assigned to the Fourth Wing, under my direct supervision."

"Fourth Wing is the vanguard," Jarek wheezed from the floor. "That's suicide."

"It's the safest place in the battle," I said, my gaze locked on Vea. "Because I will be there."

I leaned down, bringing my face level with hers.

"But know this, Little Red. If you get hurt... if you take a risk I did not authorize... I will burn this entire mountain down around our ears. Do not test me."

"I wouldn't dream of it," she lied.

I straightened up.

"Kael," I barked. "Sound the horns. Mobilize the cadets. We march at dawn."

"Yes, sir!"

I grabbed Vea's hand. "Come with me."

"Where are we going?"

"To the armory," I said, pulling her toward the door. "If you're going to fight the end of the world, you need better steel."

As we left the War Room, I felt the eyes of every commander on my back. They weren't looking at their leader anymore. They were looking at a madman who had just declared war on reality for the sake of a girl.

Let them look.

I walked Vea down the spiral stairs, the cold stone seeping into the soles of my boots. My mind raced through tactics, supply lines, aerial formations. But beneath the strategy, a single, terrifying thought looped endlessly.

They know her name.

The Fae. The Void. They knew who she was.

Which meant the prophecy wasn't just a dusty book in the library. It was active.

I squeezed her hand. She squeezed back, her grip surprisingly strong.

I would armor her in sky-iron. I would wrap her in shadow-glass. I would teach her to kill with a touch.

But deep down, in the place where the dragon slept, I knew it wouldn't be enough.

The storm was here. And for the first time in a hundred years, I wasn't sure I could weather it.

Chapter Twelve

UNSHEATHED IN SHADOW

The armory smelled of grease, cold iron, and the sudden, sharp scent of violence that followed Valdus like a cloak.

"Lift your arms," Valdus ordered.

I obeyed. There was no point in arguing with him when he was in this mood—a coiled, silent fury that had terrified the War Council into submission. He cinched the straps of the new chest plate tight enough to bruise. It wasn't standard issue leather. It was black scale, iridescent under the magelights, harvested from a shed he must have kept for decades.

"It's heavy," I grunted, the weight settling on my clavicles.

"It's dragon-glass weave," he said, moving to my vambraces. His fingers were quick, efficient, checking every buckle. "It will stop a Fae arrow. It might even stop a shadow-blade, provided you don't let them get close enough to slip it between the plates."

He stepped back, assessing me. The golden fire in his eyes dimmed, replaced by a critical, soldier's appraisal. He wasn't looking at a woman. He was checking the integrity of a fortification.

"We fly in ten minutes," he said. "Stay close to my flank. If the formation breaks, you dive. Do not try to be a hero, Vea. Just survive."

"I survived twenty years in the Lower Wards without armor," I snapped, adjusting the daggers at my hips.

" The Lower Wards had rats and thieves," Valdus said, turning for the door. "The Northern Border has things that eat screams."

*

The flight was a blur of freezing wind and grey clouds. We landed at the forward operating base just as the sun began to bleed out behind the jagged peaks of the Rift.

The camp was a disaster. Mud churned under thousands of boots. Tents sagged under the weight of wet snow. The air tasted of woodsmoke and unwashed bodies, overlying the metallic tang of fear.

Valdus didn't stop to address the troops. He carved a path through the mud, his dragon-form's residual heat making the slush steam around his boots. Soldiers scramble out of his way, saluting with trembling hands. They didn't look at me. They looked at the ground, or the sky, anywhere but at the small redhead trailing the High Commander.

He ducked into the command tent—a large, canvas structure reinforced with wooden beams against the gale.

It was freezing inside.

A single brazier struggled against the chill. A map table dominated the center, and in the corner, a pile of furs served as a bed.

One pile of furs.

Valdus dropped the heavy flap, sealing us in. The noise of the camp muffled instantly, leaving only the sound of the wind snapping the canvas and the heavy rasp of his breathing.

"Where do I sleep?" I asked, looking around the stark space.

"There." He pointed to the furs.

"And you?"

"There."

I looked at him. "There's only one bedroll, Valdus."

"We are at war, Little Red. Luxury is the first casualty." He began to unbuckle his sword belt. The heavy weapon hit the table with a clatter. "And even if there were ten beds, you would still be in mine."

My pulse jumped. "Why?"

"Because the temperature drops to twenty below at night. Your human blood will freeze. My blood runs at one hundred and three degrees." He turned to face me, his hands moving to the buttons of his tunic. "Physics, Vea. Not romance."

He stripped.

He didn't do it with any seductive intent. He removed his clothes with the weary efficiency of a man who had worn them too long. The black jacket. The linen shirt. The heavy boots. The breeches.

Everything came off.

I stood by the brazier, shivering in my armor, and I couldn't look away.

He was... devastating.

I had seen him naked before, briefly, but never like this. Never in the close, intimate gloom of a tent where I was expected to lie against him.

He was a mountain range of a man. Standing six-foot-seven, he occupied the space with an arrogant mass that shouldn't have been humanly possible. His shoulders were broad shelves of muscle, tapering down to a waist that was thick with core strength. Scars disrupted the bronze skin—white slashes from blades, ropey burns from fire, the jagged puncture marks of teeth. His body was a history book of violence, and I read every line.

My gaze traveled lower.

Thick thighs, powerful enough to crush a man's skull, supported him. Between them...

My mouth went dry.

He was heavy. Thick. Dark. Even soft, the size of him was unreasonable. If that part of him woke up, it would be a weapon in its own right. A dangerous, tearing thing.

"See something you like?"

The voice was low, vibrating through the floorboards.

I snapped my eyes up. Valdus was watching me. He hadn't covered himself. He stood with his hands on his hips, unabashed, letting me look. A dark satisfaction curled the corner of his mouth.

"I'm assessing the threat level," I managed, though my voice sounded thin.

"And?"

"High. Extremely high."

He stepped closer. The heat coming off him was a physical wave, pushing back the cold of the tent.

"Take off the armor, Vea. It's cold iron. It will suck the heat right out of you."

My fingers fumbled with the buckles. The dragon-glass weave was stiff, my hands numb.

"Let me."

He brushed my hands aside. His fingers were hot, calloused, and surprisingly gentle as he undid the straps. He stripped the armor from me, piece by piece, dropping it to the mud floor. Then the tunic. Then the breeches.

I stood before him in nothing but my smallclothes—a scrap of lace that suddenly felt like nothing at all.

His eyes tracked over me. He didn't look at my scars with pity. He looked at the muscle in my legs, the definition of my abs, the swell of my breasts. His pupils blew wide, swallowing the gold until his eyes were almost entirely black.

"You are so small," he whispered. It sounded like a complaint.

"I'm compact," I corrected, hugging my arms over my chest. The cold air bit at my skin.

"Fragile."

"I am not fragile."

"We'll see."

He reached out and hooked a finger into the waistband of my underwear. He tugged. The fabric snapped.

"Bed," he ordered. "Now."

I scrambled onto the furs. They were cold, but he followed me instantly, a massive, encroaching weight. He pulled the heavy blankets over us, sealing us into a cocoon of darkness and animal heat.

It was overwhelming.

His skin burned against mine. Every point of contact—his chest against my back, his thighs tangling with mine—sent sparks shooting through my nerves. The bond roared to life, a golden hum that drowned out the wind outside.

I tried to lie still. I tried to just breathe.

But the friction was too much.

I shifted, trying to find a comfortable position. My ass brushed against his groin.

Valdus hissed.

I froze. "Sorry."

"Don't move," he ground out.

Against my lower back, I felt him change. The soft weight hardened, expanding rapidly into iron. It pressed against me, hot and insistent.

Curiosity, dangerous and sharp, spiked in my blood. I shifted again, pressing back against him.

Valdus groaned—a deep, guttural sound that vibrated in his chest.

His hand shot out, clamping onto my hip. His fingers were long enough to span the entire bone. He didn't push me away. He pulled me closer, grinding himself against me.

"You are playing with fire, Little Red," he warned, his breath hot on the back of my neck. "And we are sitting on a powder keg."

"We might die tomorrow," I whispered. The truth of it sat heavy in the dark. "The Void doesn't take prisoners."

"I won't let you die."

"You can't promise that." I turned in his arms, facing him in the dark. I couldn't see his face clearly, just the gleam of his eyes and the hard line of his jaw. "I don't want to die wondering."

"Wondering what?"

"If you're as big as you look."

Silence stretched, thick and electric.

Valdus moved. He rolled, pinning me to the furs. His weight was crushing, but he held himself up on his forearms, creating a cage of muscle and heat.

"I will break you," he said. It wasn't a threat. It was a statement of logistics. "Look at the size of me, Vea. Look at the size of you."

"I heal fast."

"Not that fast."

I reached up. My hands traced the scars on his chest, feeling the heavy, thudding rhythm of his heart. It was beating fast—too fast. The monster was rattling the cage.

"I want this," I said. "The bond wants this."

"The bond wants to breed," he snarled. "It wants to ensure the line continues before the war ends us."

"Then let it."

I wrapped my legs around his waist. The contact was electric. I felt the head of him prod against my entrance, hot and slick and terrifyingly broad.

Valdus let out a sound that was half-prayer, half-curse.

"Fine," he growled. "But don't say I didn't warn you."

He didn't kiss me. He dropped his head to the crook of my neck, biting down on the sensitive cord of muscle there. It hurt. It grounded me.

His hand moved between us, guiding himself.

When he pushed, my eyes watered.

"Valdus," I gasped, my nails digging into his shoulders. "Wait."

He stopped instantly. He was barely an inch inside, and I already felt stretched to the limit.

"I told you," he rasped, sweat dripping from his forehead onto my chest. "Too small."

"No," I gritted my teeth. "Just... give me a second."

The bond flared. I felt his desperation, his need to be inside me, warring with his terrifying fear of hurting me. He flooded my mind with gold—reassurance, heat, pleasure.

Relax, his voice echoed in my skull. *Let me in.*

The magic lubricated the way, easing the burn. My body adjusted, softening, yielding to the invasion.

"Okay," I breathed. "Okay."

He pushed again. Slow. Agonizingly slow.

He filled me completely. He stretched me wide, filling every empty space, rewriting my internal geography. It was a sensation of absolute fullness, bordering on pain, but tipping into a blinding, white-hot pleasure.

When he was fully seated, hilt-deep, I sobbed.

Valdus froze, his muscles locking up. "Did I hurt you?"

"No," I choked out, wrapping my arms around his neck, pulling his heavy head down to mine. "You're just... so much."

"I am all yours," he whispered against my lips. "Every inch."

He began to move.

It wasn't the frantic rutting of a boy. It was the powerful, rhythmic driving of a titan. He withdrew almost completely, then thrust back in, a long, gliding stroke that hit deep inside me, touching places that had never been touched.

"Valdus!" I screamed his name, uncaring if the guards outside heard.

"Good girl," he praised, his voice rough with strain. "Take it. Take all of it."

He set a brutal pace. The friction built a fire in my belly that rivaled the dragon's flame. My hips rose to meet him, instinct taking over, matching his rhythm.

The size difference, which had terrified me, became the catalyst. I was enveloped by him. Surrounded. Consumed. His bulk shielded me from the cold, from the war, from the prophecy. There was nothing in the world but the heavy slap of skin on skin and the friction of him inside me.

"Look at me," he commanded.

I opened my eyes.

He was watching me, his face a mask of strained ecstasy. His eyes were glowing, casting a golden light on the furs.

"You are mine," he growled, driving deep. "Let the Shadow King try to take you. I will tear the throat out of the sky."

The claim shattered me.

My climax hit like a lightning strike. My body clamped down around him, milking him, spasming in violent waves of pleasure.

Valdus roared.

He drove into me three more times, hard and fast, before stiffening. He poured himself into me, his release triggering a pulse of magic that flooded my veins, hot and thick and revitalizing.

He collapsed on top of me.

I shouldn't have been able to breathe under his weight, but I had never breathed easier. I lay there, twitching in the aftershocks, slick with sweat and him.

We lay like that for a long time, the wind howling outside, the brazier popping in the corner.

Finally, Valdus rolled to the side, pulling me with him so I remained tucked against his chest. He didn't pull out. He stayed inside me, keeping the connection, keeping the seal.

He ran a hand down my spine, his touch possessive.

"Still alive?" he asked quietly.

"Barely."

He kissed the top of my head. "Sleep, Vea. Tomorrow, we bleed."

I closed my eyes, listening to the steady, powerful beat of the monster's heart, and for the first time in my life, I wasn't afraid of the dark. I was sleeping with the most dangerous thing in it.

Chapter Thirteen

SMEARED IN BLOOD AND BURIED DEEP

The battlefield didn't smell like glory. It smelled of ozone, shit, and the copper tang of blood spattered across frozen mud.

Some commanders watched the tide of war from the safety of a ridge, moving pieces on a map. I wasn't that kind of general. I was in the thick of it, a blackened blade in my hand and a scream trapped in my throat.

To my left, the Fourth Wing held the line against a phalanx of Fae shock-troopers. To my right, the siege beasts—massive, lumbering hulks of stitched flesh and void magic—were hammering against the citadel's outer wards.

But my attention wasn't on the beasts. It wasn't on the Fae.

It was on the redhead a hundred yards down the slope.

Vea.

She was a blur of violence. Too small for the armor I'd strapped her into, too fast for the heavy infantry trying to crush her. She moved like smoke in a gale, ducking under a greataxe, driving her daggers into the unarmored armpit of a soldier twice her weight.

My chest ached. A constant, dull throb behind the sternum.

Turn around, my instincts screamed. *Watch your flank.*

I decapitated a Fae soldier without looking, the black steel of my sword shearing through bone and gorget alike.

My eyes snapped back to her.

It was a sickness. A madness. Every time a blade swung near her, the breath froze in my lungs. Every time she slipped in the mud, my dragon clawed at the inside of my ribcage, demanding to be let out, demanding to wrap around her and incinerate anything that dared to exist in her vicinity.

"Valdus!" Kael's voice cut through the roar of battle. "The East Flank! The wards are failing!"

I didn't answer. I couldn't look away.

Vea had overextended.

She was chasing a retreating scout, putting distance between herself and the shield wall. It was a rookie mistake. It was a fatal mistake.

"Get back!" I roared, the command amplified by the magic in my blood. It shook the stones under my boots.

She didn't hear me. Or she ignored me.

Three Fae soldiers rose from the snow where they'd been hiding, their armor painted white to blend with the drift. They cut off her retreat.

A trap.

My heart stalled. The human part of my brain calculated the distance—too far to run. Too far to throw a blade.

The dragon brain took over.

Mine.

The word wasn't a thought. It was a geological event.

I dropped my sword. I didn't need it.

I sprinted toward the ledge overlooking her position. The air around me began to distort, heat waves shimmering off my skin, melting the snow before my boots even touched it.

"Sir!" Kael shouted. "You can't leave the command post!"

I was already gone.

I hit the edge of the cliff and jumped.

Gravity took hold, dragging me down toward the jagged rocks of the valley floor. I didn't fight it. I embraced the fall.

Break.

My bones shattered and reformed in a heartbeat. The agony was familiar, a sharp, white-hot price for power. Skin hardened into obsidian scales. Fingers lengthened into scythes. The scream of a man became the roar of a god.

I didn't fully shift—there wasn't room in the narrow valley without crushing our own troops. I became a hybrid nightmare. Twenty feet tall, bipedal, wings half-unfurled and wreathed in shadow.

I hit the ground between Vea and the soldiers.

The impact drastically altered the geography of the battlefield. Rock pulverized. A shockwave of dust and force threw the three Fae soldiers onto their backs.

Vea stumbled, shielding her face from the debris. She looked up.

Her eyes went wide. She had seen the dragon. She had seen the man. She had never seen the thing in between.

One of the Fae soldiers, a captain with silver armor and a death wish, scrambled to his feet. He lunged, not at me—he knew better—but at her. He thought he could use her as a shield.

His hand closed around her upper arm.

The world went red.

Sound vanished. Light vanished. There was only the offender and the offense.

I moved faster than a creature of my size should exist. My hand, a massive gauntlet of black scale and talon, snapped out.

I caught the Fae captain by the head.

I didn't squeeze. I didn't throw him.

I tore.

A wet, ripping sound echoed off the canyon walls. The body dropped. I held the head for a second, the expression of surprise frozen on the dead face, before crushing it into paste and discarding it.

The other two soldiers scrambled backward, dropping their weapons, their mouths open in silent screams.

I opened my mouth.

Black fire, liquid and heavy like napalm, poured out.

It washed over them. They didn't burn; they disintegrated. The fire consumed the snow, the rock, and the air itself, leaving nothing but a scorching scar on the earth.

Silence rippled outward from where I stood. Even the siege beasts seemed to pause.

I turned to Vea.

She was backed against a boulder, her daggers still in her hands, her chest heaving. Blood—not hers, thank the gods—splattered her cheek.

I dropped to one knee, the ground shaking. The scales on my face receded slightly, allowing me to speak, though my voice was a grinding of tectonic plates.

"Did they touch you?"

She stared at me. She didn't flinch. She looked at the carnage, then at the monster who caused it, and lowered her weapons.

"Just the arm," she whispered.

"Does it hurt?"

"No."

"Good."

The rage didn't subside. It curdled into something heavier, darker. The adrenaline of the kill mixed with the terror of almost losing her, creating a potent, poisonous cocktail in my blood.

I needed to get her out. Now.

I scooped her up. My hand encompassed her entire torso. She was so small. So terribly, frighteningly breakable.

I launched myself into the sky.

The wings caught the updraft, straining under the weight of my half-shifted form. We didn't go back to the command post. I couldn't be around people. I couldn't listen to logistics and casualty reports.

I needed ground. I needed dark. I needed to verify, with every sense I possessed, that she was still alive.

I flew to the upper ridges, to a small cavern set high in the granite face of the peak—a dragon-hole I used when the noise of the humans became too much.

I landed hard, skidding on the stone floor of the cave. I released Vea, setting her gently on her feet, and let the magic go.

The shift back to human was brutal. I collapsed to my hands and knees, retching, steam pouring off my naked skin. The cold air of the cave bit at me, but I burned from the inside out.

"Valdus?"

Her voice was tentative.

I looked up.

She stood near the cave entrance, silhouetted against the grey light. She was dirty, exhausted, and alive.

I stood up.

The predator was still in the driver's seat. I crossed the distance between us in two strides.

I slammed her back against the rough stone wall.

It wasn't gentle. It was desperate. My hands bracketed her head, trapping her. I buried my face in her neck, inhaling deeply. She smelled of sweat, steel, and the unique, ozone scent of her own rising magic.

"You left the formation," I growled against her throat. My teeth grazed the pulse point. "I told you to hold the line."

"They were flanking us," she argued, breathless. Her hands came up to grip my biceps, her fingers digging in. She didn't push me away. She pulled me closer. "I saw a gap."

"You saw a grave," I snarled. I pulled back to look at her. "Do you have any idea what it does to me? Watching you down there? You are a piece of glass in a rock tumbler, Vea."

"I can handle myself."

"You were three seconds away from being gutted."

"But I wasn't." She glared at me, her green eyes furious and bright. "Because you came."

"I will always come." The confession was torn from me, raw and bleeding. "That is the problem. I will burn the entire map to keep a scratch off you. Do you understand? You are making me weak."

"No," she said. She reached up, her thumb tracing the hard line of my jaw. "I'm making you use the fire."

The touch snapped the last thread of my control.

The fear of her death morphed instantly into a need to claim her life. I didn't want to talk. I didn't want to argue about tactics. I wanted to be so deep inside her that she couldn't tell where her soul ended and mine began.

I crushed my mouth to hers.

It wasn't a kiss. It was a collision. I plundered her mouth, tasting the adrenaline on her tongue. She met me with equal force, her small body arching into mine, hard angles and soft curves fitting against me like a puzzle piece.

My hands roamed over her, frantic. I needed skin.

I found the buckles of her armor. I tore them open. The leather chest piece clattered to the floor. The tunic followed.

She was fumbling with my breeches, her cold fingers grazing the heated skin of my hip.

"Valdus," she gasped, breaking the kiss. "Please."

The plea shattered me.

I lifted her.

She wrapped her legs around my waist instinctively. I carried her deeper into the cave, away from the wind, to where a pile of old furs lay in the shadows. I didn't lay her down. I pressed her against the wall again, needing the verticality, the leverage.

I kicked my breeches off.

The air was freezing, but the heat between us was a blast furnace. The bond was singing—a high, golden note of absolute rightness.

I positioned myself between her thighs. The tip of me brushed against her entrance. She was wet—slick with the arousal that danger always seemed to trigger in her.

But the size difference...

I hesitated. I looked down. I was massive. A weapon of war trying to fit into a lock made for something much smaller.

"I will hurt you," I rasped, my forehead resting against hers. Sweat dripped from my nose. "Vea, look at me. I'm too big."

"You won't," she whispered. Her hands tangled in my hair, pulling my head back so our eyes met. "The bond... it knows."

She was right. The magic swirled around us, golden light bleeding from my skin to hers. It softened her. It made her pliable.

"Good girl," I groaned, the praise slipping out unbidden. "Relax for me. Open for me."

I pushed.

Just the head.

She gasped, her nails digging into my shoulders, drawing blood. Her body was tight—impossibly tight. A velvet vice that threatened to snap my control in half.

"Valdus," she whined, her head falling back against the stone.

"I know," I murmured. I kissed her throat, licking the salt from her skin. "I've got you. Breathe."

I held still, letting her adjust. The dragon in my mind was howling, demanding I drive home, demanding I mark her. I forced the beast down. I forced myself to be the man.

"You are mine," I whispered against her skin. "Say it."

"Yours," she choked out. "I'm yours."

"Again."

"I am yours, Valdus. All of it."

The surrender was the key.

I pushed again.

Slowly. Inch by agonizing inch. I stretched her, filled her, claimed the space that no one else had ever touched.

She didn't cry out in pain. She made a sound—a low, broken keen of overwhelming sensation.

When I was fully sheathed, hilt-deep inside her, the world stopped.

The relief was narcotic. The emptiness that had plagued me for centuries vanished. I was home.

I held still for a long moment, my heart hammering against hers, savouring the absolute fullness of the connection.

"Look at me," I commanded.

Her eyes fluttered open. The pupils were blown wide, eclipsing the green.

"You take all of it," I said, a dark pride swelling in my chest. "My brave little assassin."

I began to move.

It wasn't the frantic friction of the tent. It was deep. Deliberate. I withdrew almost completely, then drove back in with a long, steady stroke that made her toes curl.

"Gods," she breathed.

"Not gods," I growled, hooking her leg higher over my hip to get deeper. "Just me."

The pace picked up. The cave echoed with the slap of skin, the heavy rasp of breath, the wet, sliding sound of our bodies.

I watched her face. I watched the way her brow furrowed, the way her lips parted. I wanted to memorize her.

The pleasure built, a dark tide rising. It wasn't just physical. The bond was wide open. I felt her pleasure as my own—a sparkling, champagne fizz in my blood. I felt her trust, terrifying and absolute.

She tightened around me, milking me with every stroke.

"Valdus, I'm close," she gasped. "I can't—it's too much."

"Let go," I ordered. I reached down, my hand finding the sensitive nub between us. I rubbed her, adding friction to the pressure. "Come for me, Little Red. Burn it down."

She shattered.

Her climax hit her like a physical blow. She screamed my name, her body clamping down on me with a strength that nearly brought me to my knees. The magic flared—blindingly bright. Shadows and gold light swirled around us, cracking the stone floor beneath my feet.

I followed her over the edge.

I buried my face in her shoulder and poured myself into her. The release was violent, a tearing of the soul. I emptied everything—the fear, the rage, the love—into her.

We stayed like that for a long time. Me pinning her to the wall, her legs wrapped around me, the only sound the wind howling outside the cave and the harsh rasp of our breathing.

Slowly, the golden light faded. The shadows retreated to the corners.

I didn't pull out. I couldn't. The thought of separating from her physically made my stomach turn.

I kissed her temple. My lips lingered on the damp hair there.

"You," I said, my voice wrecked, "are going to be the death of me."

Vea lifted her head. She looked exhausted, her lips swollen, her neck marked red from my beard burn. She looked like a ruin. A beautiful, catastrophic ruin.

"If I die," she whispered against my chest, "I want to go out like this."

"You aren't dying," I said. I pulled back slightly, brushing a strand of hair from her face. My thumb rubbed the scar on her cheek. "I just killed a captain for touching your arm. Imagine what I'll do to anyone who tries to take the rest of you."

"The battle..."

"Is still raging."

"We have to go back."

"I know."

I withdrew slowly. The loss of contact was a physical ache, a cold draft rushing into a warm room. I lowered her legs, setting her feet on the floor, but kept my arm around her waist to steady her.

She wobbled.

"Easy," I murmured.

She looked down at herself, then at me. We were both smeared with grime, sweat, and the remnants of the fight.

"We need to get dressed," she said, reaching for her tunic.

I grabbed her hand.

"Vea."

She looked at me.

"The prophecy," I said quietly. "The one about the Bloodfire Queen."

She stiffened. "What about it?"

"It says she burns the world."

I picked up her breastplate, the black scales gleaming in the dim light. I held it against her chest, my hands lingering over her heart.

"Let it burn," I said. "As long as you're the one holding the match."

She stared at me for a long beat, searching my face for any sign of hesitation. She found none.

A slow, sharp smile curved her lips. It wasn't a nice smile. It was the smile of the girl who had survived the gutters and tamed a dragon.

"Help me with the buckles, General," she said. "We have a war to win."

I turned her around and began to fasten the armor, sealing my heart inside the black steel cage of her ribs.

Chapter Fourteen

A Pyre for Every Scar

The wind screaming outside the cave mouth didn't sound like weather anymore. It sounded like a warning.

Inside, the air was thick with the scent of us—musk, sweat, and the iron tang of blood that wasn't ours. I leaned back against the rough stone wall, my legs feeling like jelly, my lungs burning with every inhale. The cold stone bit into my bare skin, but the heat radiating from the man looming over me kept the frost at bay.

Valdus pulled back, just enough to look at me.

The golden fire in his eyes had dimmed to a simmering ember. He looked wrecked. His dark hair was a mess of curls plastered to his forehead by sweat, and the scars on his chest stood out in stark white relief against his flushed skin.

He ran a thumb over my lower lip. His hand was trembling.

"You're shaking," I whispered.

"Adrenaline crash," he murmured, his voice a low rumble that vibrated through my sternum. "And terror."

"You don't get terrified."

"I do now."

He stepped away, the loss of his contact hitting me like a bucket of ice water. He moved to the pile of discarded gear, rummaging through a pack. The muscles of his back shifted and coiled, a map of power and violence. The monstrous bulk of him filled the small cavern, making the rock walls feel fragile.

He returned with a rag and a small flask. He uncorked it, pouring water onto the cloth. Steam rose instantly in the freezing air.

"Arm," he ordered.

I held out my arm. Dried blood crusted the skin from elbow to wrist—splatter from the Fae captain he'd torn apart.

Valdus gripped my wrist. His fingers were gentle, terrifyingly so, considering what I'd just seen them do. He wiped the blood away with slow, deliberate strokes. He didn't just clean me; he purified me. He scrubbed until the skin was raw and pink, until every trace of the enemy was erased.

"It's not my blood, Valdus."

"I know," he gritted out, not looking up. "But it touched you. I don't like it."

"You can't scrub the war off me."

"Watch me."

He moved to my neck, wiping away the grime and sweat. The rough cloth dragged across my sensitive skin, followed by the cool air. I shivered.

He stopped. He dropped the rag and Cupped my face in both hands, forcing me to look at him.

"I never wanted this," he said, the confession stark and bleeding. "I spent a century building walls. I made myself into a weapon that had no handle, no trigger that anyone else could pull. I was safe because I was alone."

His thumbs brushed my cheekbones.

"Now..." He shook his head, a dark laugh escaping him. "Now I am a exposed nerve. When that captain grabbed you... the world went red, Vea. I didn't make a tactical decision to shift. I didn't think about the chain of command or the structural integrity of the valley. I just knew that if I didn't end him, I would burn the sky until it collapsed."

My heart hammered against my ribs. The bond hummed between us, a live wire transmitting his residual panic. It was a heavy, suffocating weight.

"You saved me," I said.

"This time." His hands tightened on my face. "But what about next time? What about when the Void moves against us? I can't be everywhere. And knowing that—knowing there is a version of tomorrow where you don't exist—it paralyzes me."

"Then don't be paralyzed," I said, covering his hands with mine. My fingers looked like children's toys against his knuckles. "Be angry. Be the monster they're afraid of."

"I am the monster," he whispered. "But you are the leash. And if the leash snaps..."

He didn't finish. He didn't have to.

He leaned down and kissed me. It wasn't the desperate, devouring kiss of before. It was a seal. A promise. It tasted of salt and finality.

"Get dressed," he said against my lips, pulling away. "The Fourth Wing needs its commander. And I need to remind Jarek why he doesn't give me orders."

*

Putting the armor back on felt like stepping into a coffin.

The black scale chest plate was cold and stiff. Valdus helped me with the buckles, his movements efficient and soldierly, the lover tucked away behind the mask of the General. But every time his knuckles grazed my skin, sparks danced along my nerves.

He strapped his own sword belt on, the heavy black steel settling on his hips. He threw the fur cloak over his shoulders, instantly transforming from the wild creature in the cave back into the High Commander of the Sky Legion.

"Ready?" he asked.

I checked my daggers. "Ready."

We stepped out of the cave. The wind hit us instantly, a physical blow that tried to knock me off the ledge. Valdus stepped in front of me, acting as a windbreak.

He looked over the edge. Far below, the battle was a chaotic smear of movement in the mud. Smoke rose in black columns, mixing with the low, grey clouds.

"Get on."

He didn't shift fully. He dropped into a crouch, and the magic cracked around him like lightning. Bones crunched, skin hardened, and the massive black dragon exploded outward. It was faster this time, fueled by the urgency of the war below.

He lowered his wing for me.

I climbed up, settling into the hollow between his neck spines. The heat coming off his scales soaked through my breeches, grounding me.

Hold tight, Little Red, his voice echoed in my skull. *We are going to make an entrance.*

He launched us off the cliff.

We didn't just fly; we fell with style. He tucked his wings and dove, a black thunderbolt aimed straight for the command post. The wind roared, tearing at my eyes, but I didn't close them. I watched the ground rush up to meet us.

At the last second, Valdus snapped his wings open.

The air displacement was violent. It flattened the tents near the landing zone and sent a spray of mud and snow fifty feet into the air. He slammed into the earth, the impact shaking the teeth in my head.

He roared.

It was a sound that bypassed the ears and went straight to the hindbrain. It was a declaration of dominance. A challenge to the Fae, to the Void, to the incompetence of his own council.

I slid down his wing before he started to shift.

Soldiers were running toward us—medics, runners, guards. But they stopped ten yards out.

They stopped because of Valdus, who was currently reforming from a mountain of black scales into a man. But they looked at me.

Their eyes were wide, white-rimmed circles of fear.

I stood in the mud, my armor ill-fitting, my red hair a tangled mess, looking like I'd been dragged through a hurricane. But they didn't see a gutter rat anymore.

They saw the woman who had made the High Commander abandon his post. They saw the woman who had triggered a transformation so violent it had reshaped the battlefield.

They saw the trigger.

Valdus finished shifting. He stood up, ignored the cloak Kael tried to hand him, and stalked to my side. He didn't touch me, but he placed himself just slightly in front of me, shielding me from the rest of the camp.

"Report," he barked.

Kael stepped forward, his face pale. He glanced at me, then quickly back to Valdus.

"The immediate assault is broken, sir. The Fae pulled back when... when you engaged the captain. The sheer destructive force spooked them. They're regrouping at the ridge."

"Casualties?"

"Moderate. Fourth Wing took the brunt of it before you arrived." Kael hesitated. "General Jarek is demanding your arrest."

Valdus laughed. It was a dry, humorless sound.

"Is he?"

"He says you abandoned the command structure. He says you prioritized a single cadet over the integrity of the line."

"He's right," I said quietly.

Valdus turned his head, pinning me with a look sharp enough to cleave bone. "Quiet."

"He is right, Valdus. You left the center open."

"I closed the flank."

"You came for me."

"Same thing," he growled. He turned back to Kael. "Where is Jarek?"

"In the strategy tent. He's drafting the court martial papers."

"Excellent. I need kindling."

Valdus started walking. The sea of soldiers parted instantly. No one saluted. They just got out of the way. I followed in his wake, feeling the heavy gaze of a thousand men on my back.

We entered the strategy tent.

The atmosphere was poisonous. Jarek stood at the table, surrounded by three other commanders. They stopped talking the moment Valdus entered.

Jarek looked up. His face was purple with rage.

"You," he spat, pointing a shaking finger at Valdus. "You are relieved of command. I have witnesses. You abandoned your post to save a whore."

The air in the tent dropped twenty degrees.

Valdus didn't shout. He didn't attack. He walked to the table, picked up the pitcher of wine, and poured himself a cup. His hand was perfectly steady.

"She is not a whore, Jarek," Valdus said softly, taking a sip. "She is the only reason you are currently breathing."

"Excuse me?"

"If she dies," Valdus said, setting the cup down, "I stop caring about this army. I stop caring about the Citadel. I stop caring about the Empire."

He leaned forward, placing his hands on the map. The paper began to smoke under his palms.

"If she dies, the only thing I will care about is how fast I can burn this continent explicitly to ash to ease my own grief. So, technically, by saving her, I saved all of you."

Silence stretched, tight and brittle.

"You're insane," Jarek whispered. "The bond has driven you mad."

"Maybe," Valdus agreed. He looked at me.

I stood by the entrance, my hand on my dagger. I didn't look away. I couldn't.

"But here is the new reality, gentlemen," Valdus continued, addressing the room. "Vea is not a cadet anymore. She is not a subordinate. She is my second. Where she goes, the dragon goes. If you want air support, you protect her. If you want the fire, you ensure the spark survives. Do we understand each other?"

The commanders looked at Jarek, then at Valdus, then at the smoking handprints on the map.

"Understood, High Commander," one of them murmured.

Jarek threw his quill down. "The Council will hear of this."

"Let them," Valdus said. "Tell them to bring water."

He walked over to me. He didn't ask if I was okay. He grabbed my hand, interlacing our fingers. His palm was rough, hot, and calloused.

"Come," he said. "We need to eat."

He pulled me out of the tent, back into the mud and the cold.

We walked toward his quarters in silence. The camp was busy—wounded being carried on stretchers, weapons being sharpened, pots of stew bubbling over fires. But a bubble of silence moved with us.

I looked at our joined hands.

"You just committed treason," I said.

"I committed to you."

"They're afraid of me."

"Good." Valdus looked straight ahead, his jaw set. "Fear keeps people honest."

"They think I'm a witch who ensnared you."

"Let them think what they want." He squeezed my hand. "Better they think you're a witch than a victim. Victims get eaten. Witches get respect."

We reached his tent. He held the flap open for me.

I stepped inside. The air was still warm from the brazier, the furs on the bed rumpled from where we had been earlier. It felt like a lifetime ago.

Valdus followed me in, sealing the world out.

He unbuckled his sword belt and let it drop to the floor with a heavy clatter. He sat on the edge of the bed, burying his face in his hands.

For a moment, he looked mortal. Just a man carrying the weight of the sky.

I walked over to him. I stood between his spread knees.

He looked up. The gold in his eyes was fractured, swirling with exhaustion.

"I can't do it again, Vea," he whispered. "I can't watch you almost die. It... it breaks something inside me."

I ran my fingers through his dark hair, scratching lightly at his scalp. He leaned into the touch, his eyes fluttering shut.

"You won't have to," I said.

"You can't promise that. War doesn't keep promises."

"No," I agreed. "But I can promise you this. I won't be the victim anymore. You said I was a weapon? Then sharpen me. Don't shield me, Valdus. Teach me. Make me into something that can survive you."

He wrapped his arms around my waist, pulling me close until my stomach pressed against his face. He inhaled deeply, breathing me in.

"I will," he vowed, his voice muffled against my tunic. "I will make you so dangerous that even the Void hesitates to touch you."

He pulled back, looking up at me. The resolve in his face was terrifying.

"But tonight," he said, "I just need to know you're here. Warm. Alive."

"I'm here."

He pulled me down onto his lap. The armor dug into us, but neither of us cared. We sat there in the dim light of the tent, the monster and his spark, listening to the wind howl outside.

The prophecy loomed over us like a guillotine blade. The War Council was sharpening its knives. The Fae were massing at the ridge.

But as Valdus rested his chin on my shoulder, his massive hand covering my heart to feel it beat, I realized something that terrified me more than any dragon.

I would burn the world for him, too.

The realization settled in my chest, heavy and hot. I wasn't just the weakness. I was the match. And as I looked at the map pinned to the tent wall, at the encroaching darkness of the Rift, I felt a strange, cold calm.

Let them come. Let the Fae bring their darkness. Let the Council bring their politics.

I leaned back against the solid wall of Valdus's chest, closing my eyes, and for the first time, I didn't pray for survival.

I prayed for fire.

Chapter Fifteen

The Blade Beneath the Vow

The morning light in the command tent was grey and unforgiving. It filtered through the heavy canvas, illuminating dust motes that danced in the cold air, settling on the maps, the weapons, and the woman sleeping on the furs.

I stood by the map table, my hands gripping the edge of the wood hard enough to splinter it.

Vea was asleep. Finally.

She lay curled on her side, one hand tucked under her cheek, the other resting near the dagger she insisted on keeping beneath the pillow. Her red hair was a chaotic spill of fire against the dark bear pelts. In sleep, the hard lines of her face softened. The furrow between her brows—a permanent fixture since the moment we met—smoothed out.

She looked small. Fragile.

My dragon paced inside my chest, a restless, hulking weight that scratched against the back of my ribs. *Mine,* it hissed. *Hoard her. Hide her. Burn the rest.*

I forced the beast down.

Just yesterday, I had torn a High Fae captain apart for touching her arm. The violence of it still hummed in my blood, a dark, narcotic high. I had exposed my throat to the Council, committed treason, and reshaped the landscape of the valley, all to keep this single, furious creature breathing.

But looking at her now, I didn't feel safe.

I felt the blade beneath the vow.

She wasn't just my mate. She was a survivor of the Lower Wards. She was a creature forged in neglect and sharpened by cruelty. And while the bond between us was a raging river of gold and heat, there were parts of her she kept walled off. Iron gates I couldn't batter down.

She muttered something in her sleep, her fingers twitching.

I moved before I thought about it. I crossed the small space and knelt beside the furs. I didn't touch her—not yet. I just needed to be close. I needed to smell the ozone and rain scent of her skin to verify she was real.

Her eyes snapped open.

There was no transition from sleep to wakefulness. One second she was out; the next, she was a loaded weapon. Her hand flashed to the pillow, drawing the dagger.

The tip stopped an inch from my throat.

I didn't flinch. I just looked at her.

"Easy, Little Red," I murmured, my voice rough with morning overuse. "I'm not the enemy."

She blinked, the fog of sleep clearing. Her pupils, dilated and black, constricted as she focused on me. She lowered the blade, but she didn't sheath it.

"You move too quietly," she whispered, her voice a rasp.

"I'm a predator, Vea. It comes with the territory."

She sat up, the furs falling away to reveal the simple linen tunic she wore. It was mine. It hung off one of her shoulders, exposing the pale curve of her collarbone and the fresh, angry bruise where her armor had dug in yesterday.

I reached out, tracing the purple mark with my thumb.

"Does it hurt?"

"Only when I breathe." She tried to smile, but it didn't reach her eyes.

She wasn't looking at my face. Her gaze dropped, traveling over me with a slow, deliberate intensity that made the air in the tent suddenly too thin.

I wasn't wearing a shirt. I hadn't bothered. The cold didn't touch me the way it touched others.

Her eyes tracked the scars on my chest, white slashes against bronze skin. She watched the way my pectorals shifted as I breathed, the heavy rise and fall of muscle. Her gaze moved to my arms, tracing the thick, ropey veins that traversed my biceps and forearms, leading down to my hands.

She stared at my hands. They were resting on my knees, massive and capable of terrible things.

"You are ridiculous," she murmured, a flush rising on her neck.

"Is that a complaint?"

"It's an observation." She reached out, placing her small, calloused hand over mine. Her fingers barely spanned my knuckles. "Look at the size of you. You're built like a siege engine. Every part of you is designed to break things."

"Not everything," I said, turning my hand to lace our fingers together.

"Yes. Everything." Her thumb rubbed against the palm of my hand, right over the callous formed by a century of holding a sword. Her eyes were dark, heavy with a hunger she refused to voice. "Even your softness is hard, Valdus. You're nothing but leverage and force. It makes me want to..."

She trailed off, biting her lip.

"Want to what?" I leaned in, the bond flaring hot and gold between us.

"Climb you," she admitted, the words barely audible. "Like a mountain. And see if I can make the summit shake."

heat pooled low in my gut. My dragon roared its approval.

"You shook the summit yesterday," I growled, leaning forward until our foreheads touched. "You brought the mountain down."

"General?"

The voice outside the tent was hesitant. Terrified.

I closed my eyes, a low snarl vibrating in my throat.

"What?" I barked, not moving away from Vea.

"Lieutenant Kael sent me, sir. The prisoner... the Fae General. He's awake. And he's talking."

The atmosphere in the tent shifted instantly. The intimacy evaporated, replaced by the cold, sharp edge of duty.

Vea pulled back. Her eyes were hard again. Green flint.

"I'm coming with you," she said.

"No." I stood up, grabbing my tunic from the chair. "He is a High Fae Lord. He plays mind games that can flay a human psyche. You stay here."

"I am not human anymore, Valdus. I am a dragon rider." She threw the furs off and stood. She looked ridiculous in my oversized shirt, but the set of her jaw was pure steel.

"And he is part of the army that wants to trade me for a ceasefire. I have a right to look him in the eye."

I paused, my shirt half-buttoned.

I looked at her. Really looked at her. She wasn't asking for permission. She was informing me of her movements. If I locked her in here, she would cut her way out the back.

"Fine," I said, grabbing my sword belt. "But you do not speak to him. You do not engage with his glamour. You listen. You watch. And if I tell you to leave, you leave. Do we have an accord?"

She pulled on her breeches, hopping on one foot to get them over her hips.

"We have an accord."

We didn't. I knew it. She knew it. But we strapped on our weapons and walked out into the snow anyway.

*

The temporary brig was a nightmare carved into the permafrost.

We had utilized an old mining shaft at the edge of the camp, reinforced with iron bars and anti-magic wards. It smelled of wet earth, ammonia, and the unique, sickly-sweet rot of Fae blood.

Water dripped from the ceiling, echoing in the darkness.

Kael met us at the entrance. He looked pale, his hand resting nervously on the hilt of his sword.

"He's in the lower chamber, sir. We've bound him in cold iron and suppression cuffs. He shouldn't be able to access the Void."

"Shouldn't isn't won't," I muttered, ducking my head to enter the tunnel.

Vea followed close on my heels. I could feel her anxiety through the bond—a staticky buzz against my mind—but outwardly, she was calm.

We descended.

The prisoner was chained to the rock wall at the end of the drift.

Lord Vane.

Even in rags, covered in filth, he looked regal. His skin was the color of moonlight, his hair a curtain of silver. His eyes were entirely black—no whites, no iris. Just two pools of ink.

He looked up as we approached. A slow, bloody smile spread across his face.

"The Dragon," Vane rasped. His voice sounded like dry leaves skittering on pavement. "And his... pet."

I stopped five feet from him. The urge to burn him was overwhelming. My hands heated up, smoke curling from my fingertips.

"You have information," I said, my voice echoing off the damp walls. "About the Void. About the prophecy."

Vane laughed. It was a wet, gurgling sound.

"Prophecy?" He tilted his head, his black eyes fixing on Vea. "Is that what you call it? I call it a receipt. A bill coming due."

Vea stepped out from behind me.

"Don't," I warned.

She ignored me. She walked until she was just out of his reach.

"Why do you want me?" she asked. Her voice didn't shake. "Your courier said I belong to the Shadow King. Why?"

Vane looked at her. His expression shifted from arrogance to something colder. Recognition.

"Look at you," he whispered. "You have her jaw. But you have his fire."

"Whose?" Vea demanded.

"Your parents."

The air in the tunnel went still.

Vea froze. "My parents were nobodies. Drunks in the Lower Wards who left me in a basket by the tannery."

"Is that the story?" Vane chuckled, the sound grating on my nerves. "How... charitable. It saves the Empire so much embarrassment."

"Stop talking," I said. My voice was low, dangerous. I felt a cold knot forming in my stomach. A memory, scratching at the door.

"Why should I?" Vane looked at me, his eyes gleaming with malice. "The girl deserves to know her heritage. She isn't a gutter rat, General. She is the daughter of Aelric and Siera."

The names hit me like a physical blow.

The breath left my lungs.

Aelric. The Fire-Mage who led the separatists in the Western Reach. Siera. The woman who could sing storms into existence.

Twenty years ago. The Gray Ward Uprising.

"I see you remember," Vane purred, watching the color drain from my face.

"Remember what?" Vea looked between us, panic rising in her voice. "Valdus? Who are they?"

"Traitors," I said automatically. The word tasted like ash.

"Freedom fighters," Vane corrected. "They sought to break the magical monopoly of the Dragon Riders. They wanted to teach the common folk how to harness the ley lines. A noble goal. But the King didn't like it. He called it heresy."

He leaned forward against his chains, the iron clinking.

"Tell her, Valdus. Tell her what happened to the Gray Ward."

"Shut your mouth," I roared. I stepped forward, grabbing Vane by the throat. My hand sizzled against his skin.

"Do it," Vane wheezed, smiling through the pain. "Kill me. But she will still know. She can see it in your eyes."

"Let him go!" Vea shouted.

I didn't move.

"Valdus!" She grabbed my arm. She didn't use strength; she used the bond. She sent a spike of pure, commanding will into my mind. *Let him go.*

I released him. Vane slumped back against the wall, coughing.

"They didn't abandon you, little Ember," Vane gasped, wiping black blood from his lip. "They hid you. In a basket. Under the floorboards of the safehouse. Just before the roof came down."

Vea was trembling. She stared at the Fae, her face pale as the snow outside.

"The roof?" she whispered.

"Fire," Vane said softly. "Dragon fire. Black fire. It burns hot enough to melt stone. It leaves nothing behind. Not bodies. Not bones. Just... silence."

He looked at me.

"There is only one dragon capable of that kind of heat."

Vea turned.

The movement was slow. heavy.

She looked at me. Her green eyes were wide, searching my face, begging me to deny it.

"Valdus?"

I couldn't breathe. The tunnel felt like it was shrinking, the stone walls pressing in to crush me.

"The Gray Ward," I said, my voice devoid of inflection. "Twenty years ago. The King ordered a purge of the separatist cell."

"You were there?" she asked.

"I led the raid."

"Did you... did you know about the child?"

"No." I stepped toward her, my hands raising in a gesture of surrender I had never used before. "Vea, the intel was specific. It was a military target. A stronghold. We were told there were no civilians."

"But there were," Vane interjected from the shadows. "There always are."

"You burned it," Vea whispered. She backed away from me. One step. Two.

"I followed orders," I said. The excuse sounded weak even to my own ears. It was the shield I had hidden behind for a century. *I am the weapon. I do not aim; I only strike.*

"My parents," she said, her voice cracking. "You killed them."

"I killed the rebels," I insisted, desperation clawing at my throat. "I didn't know who they were to you. I didn't know *you* existed."

"Would it have mattered?"

The question hung in the damp air.

I opened my mouth to lie. To say yes, of course, I would have stopped. I would have defied the King.

But I couldn't lie to her. The bond wouldn't let me.

Twenty years ago, I was a different monster. Colder. Hollower. If the King had ordered me to burn a cradle to stop a war, I might have done it.

My silence was the answer.

Vea let out a sound—a small, broken noise that hurt worse than any blade.

She looked at her hands. Then she looked at mine. The same hands she had praised this morning. The hands she had said were built to break things.

"I slept in the bed of my parents' executioner," she said dully.

"Vea, listen to me—"

"Don't." She held up a hand. "Do not touch me."

The rejection hit the bond like a hammer.

A crack appeared in the golden connection between us. It wasn't a physical break, but a muffling. A wall of ice slamming down. I felt her pull away, retreating deep into her own mind, shutting me out.

She turned to Vane.

The Fae Lord was watching us with glee. He had lost the war, but he had won the battle.

"You knew," Vea said to him. "That's why you wanted me here. To break us."

"The prophecy says the Bloodfire Queen dies when her mate dies," Vane said, shrugging. "But it doesn't say I have to kill him with a sword. Sometimes, you just have to kill the heart. The body follows."

Vea stared at him for a long moment. Her face hardened. The grief was still there, but she shoved it down, burying it under layers of rage.

She drew her dagger.

I tensed. "Vea—"

She didn't look at me. She stepped up to Vane.

"You think this breaks me?" she asked softly.

"It should."

"You forgot one thing, Lord Vane." She leaned in close. "I'm not just their daughter. I'm his student."

She moved too fast for him to react.

She drove the dagger into his chest. Not a fatal blow—she missed the heart intentionally—but she twisted.

Vane screamed.

"That," she whispered, "was for my mother."

She pulled the blade out.

"And this..." She looked at me then. Her eyes were dead. "This is for me."

She sheathed the dagger.

"Finish him, Valdus," she ordered. Her voice was cold. Military. "He has no more use."

She turned and walked out of the cell. She didn't look back.

I stood there, frozen.

The bond was silent. Static.

I looked down at Vane. He was clutching his chest, wheezing, black blood bubbling between his fingers. He looked up at me, his eyes full of pain and triumph.

"She will never forgive you," he gargled. "Every time you touch her... she will smell the smoke."

"I know," I said.

My dragon surfaced. It didn't roar. It didn't rage. It simply wanted to end the thing that had hurt her.

I summoned the fire. Not the yellow flame of a campfire, but the black, consuming void of the dragon's breath. It coated my hand, eating the light in the room.

"Goodbye, Vane."

I placed my hand on his face.

He didn't have time to scream.

The heat was absolute. In seconds, there was nothing left of the Fae Lord but a pile of ash and the smell of ozone.

I stood in the silence of the tomb I had made.

My hands were shaking. Not from the kill. Killing was easy. Killing was breathing.

I was shaking because, for the first time in a hundred years, I was truly afraid.

I had burned the world to save her yesterday. But twenty years ago, I had burned her world to save a kingdom that didn't deserve it.

And I knew, with the terrifying certainty of a tactician looking at a losing board, that this was a wound my magic couldn't heal.

I walked out of the cell, leaving the ash behind, and stepped into the cold light where my mate was waiting to look at me with the eyes of a stranger.

Chapter Sixteen

DISTANCE MEASURED IN SCARS

The bond was a severed nerve.

It didn't scream anymore. It just throbbed—a dull, phantom ache behind my sternum where Vea used to be.

I stood in the shadows of the archway overlooking the exorbitant waste of stone the Council called a training pit. Rain lashed against the open ceiling, mixing with the sweat and sawdust below, turning the floor into a slick trap. It was three hours past midnight. The citadel slept. The dragons slept. Even the rats in the larder had likely bedded down.

But she was there.

Vea moved like a flicker of flame in a drafty hall—erratic, dangerous, and impossibly small against the grey stone.

She wasn't sparring. Sparring implied a partner, a lesson, a goal. This was an exorcism.

She drove her elbow into the wooden throat of the training dummy. The wood splintered with a wet *crack* that echoed off the walls. She didn't stop. She spun, using the momentum to drive a heel into the dummy's midsection, tearing the burlap open and spilling sand onto the wet stone.

My beast paced behind my ribs, clawing at the obsidian cage of my restraint. It didn't understand why the mate was separate. It didn't understand the concept of guilt or the history of the Gray Ward. It only knew that the little redhead was in distress, and I was doing nothing to stop it.

Mine, the dragon hissed, its voice a grinding of tectonic plates in my mind. *Go to her.*

"No," I whispered to the empty air.

I couldn't go to her. I was the reason she was bleeding.

I leaned my shoulder against the cold stone of the archway, crossing my arms over my chest. The movement pulled the fabric of my tunic tight across the fresh burns on my arm—a parting gift from the Fae Lord I'd turned to ash yesterday. The pain was grounding. It was the only thing I felt that wasn't centered on her.

Down in the pit, Vea stopped.

She stood amidst the wreckage of three destroyed dummies, her chest heaving. The rain plastered her red hair to her skull, dark as blood in the dim torchlight. She wore only a thin undershirt and breeches, soaked through, revealing the sharp, starved angles of her scapulae.

Steam rose from her skin.

Not the steam of exertion. This was different. It curled off her shoulders in thick, grey wisps, smelling of ozone and sulfur.

Her magic was leaking.

The bond, despite her walling it off, transmitted a spike of raw, unadulterated self-loathing so potent it nearly brought me to my knees. She hated me. But gods, she hated herself more for ever trusting me.

She screamed.

It wasn't a word. It was a sound of pure frustration. She threw her hands out.

Shadows erupted from her palms.

They didn't act like normal shadows. They were solid, violent things—tendrils of darkness that lashed out like whips. They struck the stone wall ten feet away, gouging deep trenches into the granite. The impact shook the foundation of the balcony I stood on.

I gripped the railing, the stone crumbling to dust under my fingers.

She was losing control. The container was too small for the power I had awakened in her. If she kept this up, she wouldn't just break the training equipment; she would level the north tower.

I didn't make a decision to move. Gravity simply shifted.

I vaulted over the railing.

The drop was forty feet. I didn't use my wings. I didn't use magic to slow my descent. I needed the impact. I needed the jar to my bones to remind me I was still solid, still real, and not just a ghost haunting her life.

I landed in the center of the ring, crouching to absorb the force. The wet stone cracked under my boots, spiderwebbing outward.

Vea spun around.

She didn't look surprised. She looked ready.

Her green eyes were wide, the pupils blown so large the iris was barely visible. Dark veins crawled up her neck, pulsing with the erratic rhythm of her destabilized magic.

"Get out," she rasped. Her voice was wrecked, raw from screaming or crying or both.

I straightened to my full height. I let my own power bleed out, just enough to shield me from the rain, creating a dry circle around us.

"You're going to bring the tower down, Vea."

"Good," she spat. "Let it fall."

"There are cadets sleeping two floors up."

"Then evacuate them." She wiped rain from her eyes, smearing dirt across her cheek. "Go be a hero, General. That's what you do, isn't it? You save the Empire. No matter how many cradles you have to burn to do it."

The words were precision strikes. She knew exactly where the armor ended.

"I am not here to fight you," I said, keeping my voice low, devoid of the thunder that wanted to roll.

"Then why are you here?" She stepped toward me. The shadows around her hands coiled tighter, hissing like vipers. "Did you come to finish the job? Did you miss a spot twenty years ago?"

"I came to stop you from killing yourself."

"Maybe I want to die."

"Liar."

I took a step forward. The water on the floor hissed, evaporating instantly near my boots.

"You don't want to die, Vea. You want to hurt. You want to bleed so the physical pain drowns out the noise in your head. You want to exhaust yourself so you don't have to dream about the fire."

She flinched.

"Don't you dare get inside my head," she warned, backing away.

"I don't have to," I said, tapping my own temple. "You're already in mine. You're screaming in there, Little Red. It's loud."

"Then sever it!" She swung her arm, and a lash of shadow snapped at my feet. "Cut the bond! You're the High Commander. You're the strongest thing in the sky. Fix it!"

"I can't."

"Won't!"

"Can't!" I roared, the control slipping. My voice bounced off the stone walls, shaking dust from the rafters. "It is not a rope, Vea. It is a fusion. If I cut it, I lobotomize us both. Is that what you want? To be a husk?"

She stared at me, her chest rising and falling rapidly. The rain dripped from her nose, her chin. She looked wild. Ruined. Beautiful in a way that made my teeth ache.

"I want to not feel you," she whispered. "I want to wake up and not know exactly where you are. I want to not crave the skin of the man who murdered my mother."

The admission hung between us, heavy and toxic.

It was the crave that killed her. I felt it too. Even now, with hate rolling off her in waves, the magnetic pull was absolute. My body wanted to bridge the distance. My hands wanted to span her waist. My blood wanted to mix with hers until the history didn't matter.

"Then fight me," I said.

Her eyes snapped to mine. "What?"

"You have too much energy. It's poisoning you. Burn it off." I spread my arms wide, leaving my chest wide open. A target. "Hit me."

She hesitated. "I'll kill you."

"You can try."

A dark, dangerous smile touched her lips. It wasn't happy. It was the smile of a predator recognizing prey that had volunteered to be eaten.

"Draw your sword, Valdus."

"I don't need steel for you."

It was the wrong thing to say. Or the right thing, if the goal was violence.

She moved.

She was faster than she had been yesterday. The bond was augmenting her speed, feeding her my own strength even as she tried to reject it. She blurred across the wet stone, closing the twenty feet between us in a heartbeat.

She didn't use the shadows. She used her body.

She feinted left, dropped low, and swept my legs.

I didn't fall, but I staggered. Before I could recover, she drove a fist into my kidney.

It hurt. It actually hurt.

I spun, grabbing for her, but she was already gone, ducking under my arm. She jumped, landing on my back, her arm locking around my throat.

"Choke," she hissed in my ear.

She squeezed. Her arm was a band of iron. She was using magic to enhance her muscles.

I reached back, gripping the front of her tunic, and threw her.

She didn't crash. She twisted in the air, cat-like, and landed in a crouch. She launched herself back at me instantly.

This time, the shadows came with her.

A tendril of darkness wrapped around my ankle, jerking my foot back. I went down to one knee. Vea was there, her knee driving toward my face.

I caught her knee in my palm. The impact cracked the stone beneath me.

I shoved her back. She skidded across the wet floor, using her fingers to claw into the stone and stop her momentum.

"Is that it?" I goaded, standing up. I wiped a streak of mud from my jaw. "Is that all the rage you have? Your mother deserves better than that."

Her eyes went pitch black.

The air pressure in the pit dropped. My ears popped.

"Don't," she said, her voice layering over itself—part human, part dragon, part void. "Speak. Her. Name."

She held out both hands.

A spear of pure, condensed shadow formed in the air. It wasn't the smoky, insubstantial stuff from before. It was solid jagged darkness, humming with lethal intent.

She hurled it.

It moved faster than an arrow.

I didn't dodge. I couldn't dodge—it would have hit the support pillar behind me.

I caught it.

My hand closed around the shaft of the shadow-spear inches from my chest. The magic bit into my palm, cold as the void between stars. It sizzled against my skin, fighting me, trying to drill into my heart.

The pain was exquisite.

I crushed it. The spear shattered into black smoke that dissipated in the rain.

Vea didn't stop. She summoned another. And another.

She unleashed a barrage of violence. I stood my ground, batting them aside, catching them, absorbing the impacts with my forearms. My tunic shredded. Cuts opened on my arms and chest, bleeding gold-tinged blood that hissed when it hit the wet floor.

"Fight back!" she screamed, hurling a ball of grey fire that singed my eyebrows. "Damn you, Valdus! Fight back!"

"No."

I walked toward her.

She threw everything she had. Shadow whips. Force blasts. Daggers of ice.

I took it all.

A shadow-whip laid my cheek open. I didn't flinch. A blast of force hit me in the solar plexus, bruising ribs. I kept walking.

I was the mountain. She was the storm. And the storm always breaks against the mountain eventually.

She was panting now. The magic was sputtering. Her hands shook uncontrollably.

I reached her.

She swung a fist at my face. It was slow. Clumsy with exhaustion.

I caught her wrist.

She swung the other. I caught that one too.

I pinned her wrists to her sides, stepping in close until our bodies were pressed together. She struggled, thrashing against me, headbutting my chest, kicking my shins.

"Let me go!" she sobbed. The rage was cracking, revealing the grief underneath.

"I've got you," I murmured, ignoring her struggles. "I've got you, Vea."

"I hate you." She slammed her forehead against my sternum. "I hate you so much."

"I know."

"You killed them."

"I know."

She stopped fighting. Her legs gave out.

I held her up. My hands shifted from her wrists to her waist, taking her full weight. She slid down until her knees hit the stone, dragging me down with her.

We knelt there in the mud and the rain, the citadel silent around us.

She buried her face in my ruined tunic, her hands gripping the fabric so hard her knuckles turned white. She wasn't crying—Vea didn't cry—but she was shaking with dry, racking heaves that were worse than tears.

I rested my chin on the top of her head. I smelled the rain, the sweat, and the coppery tang of my own blood on her skin.

The bond flickered.

The wall she had built didn't come down, but a door opened. Just a crack.

I felt it then. The vast, howling emptiness inside her. The fear that she was fundamentally unlovable, that everyone who touched her turned to ash.

And beneath that... the craving. The absolute, terrifying need for the heat I provided.

"You're bleeding," she mumbled against my chest.

"I heal."

She pulled back. She looked at my face. Her eyes dropped to the cut on my cheek, forcing itself closed, the skin knitting together in a glow of golden light.

She reached up. Her cold fingers brushed the blood on my jaw.

"Why didn't you stop me?"

"You needed to bleed the poison out."

"I could have killed you."

"Vea," I said softly, turning my face into her palm. "You are the only thing in this world that *can* kill me. I accepted that the moment I signed the papers to bring you here."

She stared at me, searching for the lie. She found none.

Her thumb traced the line of my lip. Her gaze was dark, conflicted. The hatred was still there, but it was cooling, hardening into something manageable like steel.

"I'm not moving back into the tent," she said.

"I know."

"I don't forgive you."

"I don't expect you to."

"But..." She looked down at the space between us, where our chests were almost touching. "The cold. It hurts. Physically."

"It's the distance," I explained. "The bond treats separation like a wound. It tries to pull the edges back together."

"How do we stop the pain?"

"We don't." I covered her hand on my face with my own. "We endure it. Until the war is done."

"And then?"

"Then you can decide if you want to drive a dagger into my heart or not. I'll sharpen it for you."

She looked at me for a long time. Then, slowly, she leaned forward.

She didn't kiss me. She pressed her forehead against mine.

The contact was electric. A jolt of energy arced between us, settling the nausea in my stomach, quieting the dragon in my mind.

"You're a monster, Valdus," she whispered.

"Yes."

"But you're my monster."

"Always."

She pulled away, the loss of contact immediate and sharp. She stood up, her legs shaky but holding. She looked down at me, the High Commander of the Sky Legion, kneeling in the mud in a shredded tunic.

"Get up, General," she said, her voice devoid of warmth but full of grit. "If the Fae attack tonight, I can't carry you."

"You'd leave me?" I stood, wincing as my bruised ribs protested.

She turned to walk toward the tunnel exit. She paused at the edge of the light.

"I'd leave you," she lied. "But I'd come back for the dragon."

She disappeared into the dark.

I stayed in the rain for a moment longer, watching the space where she had been.

The bond was still muffled, still painful. But the silence had changed. It wasn't the silence of a grave anymore. It was the silence of a held breath.

I looked down at my hands. The blood—hers and mine—had mixed together, indistinguishable in the rain.

I wiped them on my breeches and turned toward the barracks.

She hadn't forgiven me. Good. Forgiveness was soft. Forgiveness got people killed.

She hated me.

And hate... hate was a fuel that burned almost as hot as love. It would keep her warm when the winter came.

I could work with hate.

Chapter Seventeen

The Fate That Demands a Monster

The Citadel Library was not a place of learning. It was a graveyard of dangerous ideas, stacked eighty feet high in a tower that smelled of rot and thunderstorms.

I shouldn't have been there. The curfew bell had tolled hours ago, and the patrols were doubled after the Fae attack. But sleep was a foreign country I couldn't visit. Every time I closed my eyes, I saw the ash on Valdus's hands. I saw the empty space where my parents should have been.

I adjusted the grip on the dark lantern, keeping the shutter almost closed. A sliver of light cut through the gloom, illuminating the dust motes dancing in the freezing air.

My body ached. Yesterday's brawl in the pit had left me a canvas of bruises, turning yellow and purple under my tunic. But the physical pain was a mercy. It was loud enough to drown out the quiet, horrific hum of the magic in my blood.

Bloodfire.

That's what Lord Vane had called it.

I moved deeper into the stacks. The Restricted Section was guarded by a ward of woven air, but the bond—that cursed, golden chain connecting me to the High Commander—acted like a master key. The ward tasted my aura, tasted *him* on me, and dissolved with a soft hiss.

I hated it. I hated that even my rebellion was enabled by his power.

I climbed the spiral iron staircase to the upper gallery. The air here was thinner, sharper. This was where they kept the histories of the First Wars. The texts that didn't make it into the cadet curriculum.

I pulled a heavy tome from the shelf. *Lineages of the Sky.*

Dust coated my fingers. I flipped the pages, searching. Not for strategy. For names.

Aelric. Siera.

Nothing.

I shoved it back and pulled another. *The Fall of the Western Reach.*

Nothing.

My frustration mounted, a hot coal in my throat. I grabbed a third book, a black-bound volume with no title, just a sigil burned into the leather: a dragon eating its own tail.

I opened it.

The pages weren't paper; they were cured skin. The ink shimmered in the lantern light, moving slightly, as if the words were still wet.

I turned the pages, my eyes scanning the archaic script. It was a catalog of anomalies. Magical mutations.

And there, halfway through, the illustration stopped my heart.

It was a sketch of a woman. She was small, engulfed in flames that were inked in pitch black. She stood atop a mountain of skulls.

The text beneath it was short. Brutal.

The Bloodfire Queen.

Rare manifestation of the draconic line. Occurs when a human vessel carries the spirit of an Elder Wyrm without the ability to shift. The container is too small for the soul.

I traced the line of text with a trembling finger.

The magic does not vent. It builds. The vessel becomes a living bomb. When the emotional threshold is breached, the Bloodfire ignites. It does not stop until the vessel is ash, or the world is.

The book slipped from my numb fingers. It hit the floor with a heavy thud that echoed like a gunshot in the silent library.

"I wondered how long it would take you to find that."

The voice came from the shadows. Deep. Resonant. It vibrated through the floorboards and straight into the soles of my boots.

I didn't turn. I couldn't.

Valdus.

The bond, which I had been trying to ignore, suddenly flared. It wasn't the roaring fire of the battlefield. It was a low, steady heat, like the embers of a city that had already burned down.

He stepped into the ring of light.

He wasn't wearing his armor. He wore black breeches and a loose shirt, the collar open to reveal the strong column of his throat. He looked exhausted. The shadows under his gold eyes were dark enough to bruise.

He picked up the book.

His hand—so large it nearly covered the entire page—smoothed the skin-parchment. "It's a rare edition," he said quietly. "Most copies were burned three centuries ago."

"By you?" My voice sounded strange. Hollow.

"By my predecessors." He closed the book and placed it on the nearest table. He didn't look at me. He looked at the spine of the tome. "They didn't like the prophecy. It made the Dragon Riders look... fallible."

"Prophecy?" I stepped back, my back hitting the cold iron railing of the walkway. "That wasn't a prophecy, Valdus. That was a diagnosis."

He finally looked at me.

The intensity of his gaze usually stripped me bare. Tonight, it just felt heavy. Sad.

"Read the next page, Vea."

"I don't want to read anymore."

"Read it."

It was an order. The General commanding the cadet.

I stepped forward, my hands shaking. I opened the book again.

The only temperance for the Bloodfire is the Anchor. A mate of sufficient power to ground the excess energy. If the Anchor holds, the Queen survives. If the Anchor breaks...

The text trailed off into a smear of ink.

"If the Anchor breaks," Valdus finished softly, "the Queen burns the continent."

The silence stretched, tight and suffocating.

I looked at him. Really looked at him. The scars on his face. The rigid set of his shoulders. The way he stood between me and the door, not as a jailer, but as a wall.

"You knew," I whispered.

"I suspected." He leaned his hip against the table, crossing his arms. "When I felt your magic in the courtyard... the way it tasted. It wasn't normal fire. It was hungry. It felt like the Void."

"So you bound me?" Rage, hot and familiar, began to claw at my ribs. "You didn't bond with me because you wanted me. You did it to put a leash on a bomb."

"I bonded with you because my soul recognized yours," he said, his voice rough. "But yes. I kept you close because I knew what would happen if I didn't."

"You killed my parents."

"I did."

"And then you found out their daughter was a walking apocalypse, so you decided to finish the job by making her your prisoner."

"Is that what you are?" He pushed off the table, taking a step toward me. The air pressure in the gallery dropped. "A prisoner?"

"I can't leave!" I shouted. "If I go more than five miles from you, I bleed. If I try to run, you hunt me down. And now I find out that if you die, I explode? That isn't a partnership, Valdus. That's a hostage situation."

"It's survival," he growled.

He closed the distance between us. He didn't touch me, but he loomed over me, his heat radiating against my cold skin.

"Do you think I wanted this?" he demanded, his eyes flashing. "Do you think I wanted to tie my life to a woman who looks at me with her mother's eyes? A woman who hates me?"

"I don't hate you," I lied. The words tasted like copper. "I despise you. There's a difference."

"Despise me all you want." He slammed his hand against the bookshelf next to my head, boxing me in. "But you are alive. You are breathing. You are not a pile of ash in a gutter. I made a choice, Vea. I chose your life over my peace."

"My life?" I laughed, a sharp, jagged sound. "You call this a life? Waiting for the moment I lose control? Waiting for the monster to wake up?"

"The monster is already awake," he said softly. He lowered his head until his face was inches from mine. "I saw her in the pit last night. I saw her tear the training dummies apart with shadows that shouldn't exist."

My breath hitched. "I couldn't stop it."

"I know."

"It felt good." The confession slipped out, terrifying me. "It felt... right."

"I know that too."

He reached out. His fingers hovered over my cheek, hesitant. Then, slowly, he brushed a strand of hair from my face. His touch was electric, a jolt that went straight to my core.

"That is why you need me," he murmured. "I am the only thing strong enough to hold you when you break."

"And if you break?" I asked. "The prophecy says if the Anchor fails..."

"I won't fail."

"You're mortal, Valdus. You bleed. I saw you bleed."

"I am hard to kill."

"But not impossible."

I stared at his throat. The pulse beating there. Strong. Steady. If that stopped... the world ended.

The weight of it crushed me. I wasn't just a failed assassin anymore. I wasn't just an orphan. I was the trigger for a weapon that could wipe the Empire off the map. And the only safety mechanism was the man I had sworn to kill.

"Why didn't you just kill me?" I asked, my voice barely a whisper. "When you found me in the stables. When you realized what I was. It would have been safer. Cleaner."

Valdus went still. His hand froze on my cheek.

"I tried," he admitted. The words were a jagged stone in the air.

I flinched.

"I had my hand on your throat," he continued, his eyes searching mine, brutally honest. "I looked at you, and I saw the threat. I saw the Bloodfire. Logic dictated I snap your neck and save the kingdom the trouble."

"Why didn't you?"

"Because you bit me."

A dark, humorless smile touched his lips.

"You were half-starved, bleeding, terrified... and you sank your teeth into my hand. You had no chance of survival, and you chose violence anyway."

His thumb traced my lower lip.

"I couldn't kill that kind of fire, Vea. I wanted to see what it would burn."

"And now?" I asked. "Now that you know it burns everything?"

He leaned in. His forehead rested against mine.

"Now," he whispered, "I'll let it burn. As long as we burn together."

The library seemed to vanish. The musty smell of books was replaced by the scent of him—woodsmoke and rain. The fear that had been clawing at my throat softened, replaced by that treacherous, magnetic pull.

"You're insane," I breathed.

"I'm yours."

The declaration hung between us.

It wasn't romantic. It was a sentence. A condemnation.

Suddenly, the alarm bells shattered the moment.

The sound was deafening—a chaotic, clanging rhythm that meant only one thing.

Breach.

Valdus pulled back instantly. The vulnerability vanished, replaced by the mask of the High Commander.

"The wards," he snapped, turning toward the window. "They're down."

I ran to the railing.

Outside, the storm had turned green. Sorcery, thick and toxic, was pouring over the walls of the Citadel. Shadows that didn't belong to the night were scaling the stone, pulling themselves up with clawed hands.

"The Fae," I said, daggers already in my hands. "They didn't wait for the morning."

"No." Valdus drew the massive sword from the scabbard he'd left leaning against the table. The black steel hummed, drinking the light. "They came for the Queen."

He looked at me.

"Stay close to me, Vea. If you feel the fire rising..."

"I know," I said, my grip tightening on my blades until my knuckles turned white. "Don't let go."

"Never."

He kicked the library doors open and we ran into the hallway, straight into the mouth of the war he had started to save me. But as we ran, the dread in my stomach wasn't about the Fae or the battles to come.

It was the knowledge that the most dangerous thing in this castle wasn't the dragon.

It was me.

Chapter Eighteen

Making Peace with Teeth

The alarm bells didn't just ring; they screamed. The sound was a physical assault, vibrating through the iron floorboards of the library loft and rattling the teeth in my skull.

Breach.

Valdus moved instantly. The transition from vulnerable confessor to High Commander was violent in its speed. He snatched his massive black greatsword from where it leaned against the history table, the steel singing as it sliced the air.

"Move, Vea," he barked, already turning toward the double doors. "We need to get to the lower wards before—"

"No."

I didn't move toward the door. I moved toward him.

He stopped, turning back with a snarl that died halfway up his throat. The urgency of the invasion warred with the sudden, suicidal defiance in my posture.

"This isn't a debate," he growled, the gold in his eyes flaring like a forge. "The Fae are inside the walls."

"Let them come," I said. My voice was steady, terrified, and reckless. "You said I was a bomb, Valdus. You said I was going to burn the world down."

"I said I would stop it."

"You can't stop it. The book said the only temperance is the Anchor." I took another step. The distance between us was charged, the air thick enough to choke on. "Prove it."

He stared at me, his chest heaving. The leather of his jerkin strained across his shoulders, and for a second, the war outside ceased to exist. All I could see was him.

Gods, he was devastating.

He stood there, a towering monument of violence and ruin, and my treacherous body didn't care that he was a liar or a killer. I looked at the thick cords of muscle in his neck, the way his jaw set like granite, the dark shadow of stubble that would scrape my skin raw. My eyes dropped to his hands—those massive, scarred hands that could crush a skull as easily as they could turn a page. The veins on his forearms were raised, intricate maps of strength that led up to biceps thick enough to break me in half. He was death packaged in bronze skin and obsidian scales, a monster on a leash, and the hunger that spiked in my belly was so sharp it hurt.

I didn't want safety. I wanted him to ruin me before the Fae got the chance.

"Vea," he warned, his voice dropping an octave. "We don't have time."

"Make time."

I closed the gap and shoved him.

It was like shoving a wall. He didn't budge an inch, but his breath hitched. The bond between us, already agitated by the danger, snapped taut. It wasn't a golden thread anymore; it was a live wire, pumping his adrenaline into my veins and my arousal into his.

"You killed my parents," I whispered, grabbing the front of his shirt. "You bound me to a prophecy that ends in ash. You owe me this."

"I owe you survival," he rasped. "Not this."

"I don't want to survive!" I screamed, the hysteria finally cracking through. "I want to feel something other than dread! I want to know that if I burn, you're burning with me!"

Something in him shattered.

The restraint—that iron-clad control he wore like armor—disintegrated.

He dropped the sword. It hit the floor with a heavy clang that was immediately forgotten as his hands seized my waist.

He didn't pull me in; he lifted me.

I gasped as my feet left the floor. He slammed me back against the nearest bookshelf. The impact knocked the wind out of me and sent a dozen priceless historical texts tumbling to the ground. I didn't care. I wrapped my legs around his waist, desperate to anchor myself against the storm.

"You want to burn?" he snarled against my mouth, his hands bruising in their intensity. "Fine."

He didn't kiss me. He devoured me. His mouth crushed mine, teeth clashing, tongue sweeping in a claiming so absolute it bordered on violence. It tasted of copper and rage. There was no gentleness here, no romance. This was war by other means.

I clawed at his shoulders, my nails digging into the leather, seeking the skin beneath. The bond roared in my ears, a cacophony of *mine, mine, mine.*

He tore his mouth away, burying his face in the crook of my neck. He bit down on the sensitive cord of muscle there, hard enough to leave a mark that would last for weeks. I cried out, arching into him, the pain acting as a friction match to the gasoline in my blood.

"You are a plague," he groaned, his hands shifting to grip my thighs, spreading me wider. "You are going to be the death of me, Little Red."

"Good." I yanked his head up, forcing him to look at me. "Die with me."

His eyes were molten gold, the pupils blown wide, eclipsing the iris. The dragon was right there, staring out from the human mask.

He didn't waste time with buttons. He ripped the fabric of my breeches. The sound of tearing cloth was loud in the quiet gallery. His hand found me, calloused and rough and hot.

I nearly sobbed. The friction was immediate, overwhelming. He didn't tease. He didn't prepare. He touched me with the familiarity of ownership, knowing exactly where to press, where to rub, his fingers moving with a relentless, punishing rhythm.

"Wet," he growled, the word vibrating against my jaw. "You hate me, and you're soaking wet for me."

"Shut up," I panted, my hips bucking against his hand. "Just... Valdus, please."

He withdrew his hand. The loss was a physical ache.

"Say it," he demanded, his voice a low rumble that shook my bones. He adjusted himself, the heavy ridge of him pressing against my entrance. The size of him was terrifying, impossible. "Tell me who initiates the burn."

"You," I begged, digging my fingers into his hair. "You."

He drove into me.

It wasn't a slide. It was an invasion. He filled me completely, stretching me to the point of pain, a blunt, heavy force that scattered my thoughts like dry leaves in a hurricane. I screamed his name, my head falling back against the books.

"Look at me!" he ordered.

I forced my eyes open.

He was watching me. He watched every twitch of my face, every gasp, drinking in my unraveling as if it were the only water in a desert. He began to move, snapping his hips with a brutal, rhythmic efficiency.

Bam.

My back hit the books.

Bam.

The friction was agonizing, perfect. The bond flared with every thrust, sending waves of golden light pulsing through my skin. I could feel his pleasure bleeding into mine—a dark, heavy heat that pooled low in my belly. I could feel his desperation, the terror that he was going to lose me, the need to bury himself so deep that even death couldn't pry us apart.

"Mine," he gritted out, his forehead pressing against mine, sweat dripping from his temples. "The prophecy can go to hell. The Council can rot. You are mine."

"Yours," I sobbed, wrapping my legs tighter, pulling him deeper. "I'm yours."

The shadows in the room began to lengthen, twisting around us, reacting to the surge of magic. My power leaked out, uncontrolled, but Valdus didn't pull away. He drank it in. The darkness coiled around his arms, caressing his skin, merging with the obsidian scales that were starting to patch across his shoulders.

We were a catastrophe in motion.

The tension coiled tight in my lower stomach, a spring wound to the breaking point. I bit his shoulder to muffle a scream as the crest approached. He felt it—through the bond, through the way my inner muscles clamped around him—and he abandoned all rhythm, hammering into me with frantic, animalistic strokes.

"Let go," he roared.

I shattered.

It wasn't just a physical release; it was a magical detonation. Pleasure ripped through me, white-hot and blinding, followed instantly by a shockwave of shadow that blasted outward, knocking books off the shelves for twenty feet in every direction.

Valdus groaned, a sound torn from the bottom of his chest. He slammed into me one last time, burying himself to the hilt, and poured himself into me. His magic flooded my veins, hot liquid gold mixing with my shadows, grounding me, claiming me, fusing the cracked pieces of my soul back together with molten lead.

We stayed there for a long moment, suspended in the wreckage.

He held me pinned to the shelf, his chest heaving against mine, our hearts beating in a frantic, syncopated rhythm. His face was buried in my hair, his breathing harsh and ragged.

Slowly, the world filtered back in.

The smell of sex and ozone. The dust settling in the lantern light.

And the bells.

The bells were still ringing.

Valdus pulled back. He didn't step away immediately. He smoothed my hair back from my damp forehead, his touch surprisingly gentle for a man who had just ravaged me against a biography of the First Age.

"Can you stand?" he asked, his voice rough.

"Yes."

He lowered me to the floor. My legs wobbled, feeling like jelly, but I locked my knees.

We didn't speak. There was nothing to say. The hate wasn't gone—my parents were still dead, and he was still their executioner—but the frantic, clawing need had been fed. The anchor held.

He adjusted his breeches. I fixed my torn tunic as best I could, using a strip of shadow to bind the ripped fabric at my hip.

Valdus bent down and retrieved his greatsword.

When he straightened, the lover was gone. The High Commander stood in his place, cold and lethal. But when he looked at me, the gold in his eyes was solid. Unwavering.

"The Fae are likely in the Great Hall by now," he said, checking the edge of his blade.

I bent down and picked up my daggers. They felt light in my hands. My magic felt quiet, sated, coiled and ready to strike at something other than myself.

"Then we should go introduce ourselves," I said.

Valdus reached out. He didn't take my hand. He ran his thumb over my lower lip, swollen from his own mouth.

"Stay behind my shield, Vea. If you see green fire, you run."

"I don't run," I corrected him, testing the balance of my steel. "I burn."

A grim, terrifying smile touched his lips.

"Then let's go set the world on fire."

He kicked the library doors open, and we stepped out into the screaming dark.

Chapter Nineteen

THE WORLD BLEEDS FIRST

The corridor didn't look like a hallway anymore. It looked like the throat of a dying beast.

Smoke, thick and greasy, rolled along the stone ceiling, choking the torchlight. The alarm bells were no longer a rhythmic warning; they were a continuous, maddening scream that vibrated in the marrow of my bones.

Valdus didn't run. He hunted.

He moved down the center of the hall, his massive black greatsword held low, the tip carving sparks against the granite floor. I stayed in his wake, a shadow tethered to a storm.

My body still hummed with the aftershocks of the library. The magic he had poured into me wasn't settling; it was rioting. It clawed at the back of my throat, tasting like ash and iron, demanding a target. The bond between us was a live wire, stripping my nerves bare. I felt the heat of his skin from three feet away. I felt the heavy, thudding rhythm of his heart as if it were beating behind my own ribs.

Fear.

Not his. Mine.

"They're close," I said. My voice sounded scrap-metal rough.

"I know." Valdus didn't look back. His shoulders were a wall of black leather and tension. "Stay off the center line. Use the pillars."

"I'm not a cadet, Valdus."

"No. You're the target."

He stopped.

The air pressure in the corridor dropped. My ears popped.

At the far end of the hall, the shadows detached themselves from the walls. They weren't natural darkness. They were oily, incorrect things that slithered over the stone, coalescing into tall, spindly shapes.

Fae.

But not the beautiful, courtly monsters from the storybooks. These were the vanguard. They wore armor made of chitin and bone, their faces hidden behind masks of smooth, featureless silver. Green fire dripped from their weapons, sizzling where it hit the floor.

"Carrix," the lead Fae hissed. The sound was wet, like a lung filling with fluid. "The Dragon and his Whore."

Valdus didn't speak. He didn't posture.

He exploded into motion.

The violence was sudden and absolute. He closed the thirty feet between them in a blur of speed that shouldn't have been possible for a man of his size. His greatsword was a black blur, a guillotine swinging parallel to the ground.

The lead Fae tried to block. The heavy steel of Valdus's blade sheared through the creature's parry, through the bone armor, and through the torso beneath. Black blood sprayed the wall.

Two more lunged at him.

"Right side!" I screamed.

I didn't think. I didn't plan. I let the bond take the wheel.

I dove.

I slid across the polished stone, passing underneath Valdus's outstretched arm. The world narrowed to the gap in the Fae soldier's armor—the soft spot behind the knee.

My daggers bit deep.

The creature shrieked, its leg buckling.

I rolled, coming up into a crouch. Valdus was already there. He didn't look at me; he simply stepped back, his boot connecting with the falling Fae's chest, crushing the ribcage, while his sword took the head off the third attacker.

We moved as one organism.

The sex in the library had torn down the last of the barriers between our minds. I didn't need to watch him to know where he was. I felt the shift of his weight before he lunged. I felt the heat of his fire before he exhaled it. When he swung high, I went low. When I dodged left, he filled the space on my right with a wall of obsidian scales and death.

It was terrifying. It was euphoric.

A Fae with a dual-bladed staff spun toward me. The green fire on the blades crackled, smelling of rotten limes.

I parried, the impact jarring my shoulder. He was too strong. He shoved me back, raising the staff for a killing blow.

Burn.

The command wasn't mine. It came down the bond, a roar of possessive fury.

Valdus abandoned his own opponent. He reached out, his hand engulfing the Fae's face.

"Don't. Touch. Her," he snarled.

Fire—black and hungry—erupted from his palm. The Fae didn't even have time to scream. The head turned to ash instantly, the body crumpling to the floor like a puppet with cut strings.

Valdus spun, grabbing my arm. His grip was bruising, desperate.

"Are you hit?" he demanded, his eyes scanning me, wild with adrenaline.

"No." I was panting, my chest heaving. "Valdus, behind you!"

He didn't turn. He just flared his wings—phantom limbs of shadow and heat that manifested for a split second—and the blast of hot air knocked the approaching soldiers off their feet.

"We need to get to the Great Hall," he growled, pulling me against his side. "The main force is breaching the lower gates."

We ran.

The fighting grew thicker the deeper we went. The citadel was waking up. Cadets were pouring out of the barracks, half-armored, swords clashing against the invaders. Logic evaporated. The hallway became a meat grinder.

I fought with a savagery that scared me.

My shadows were no longer clumsy. They lashed out like vipers, wrapping around ankles, blinding eyes, pulling enemies onto my blades. Every time my steel drank blood, the hum in my veins grew louder, a crescendo of dark power.

Feed me, the magic whispered. *Burn it all.*

"Control it, Vea," Valdus warned, his voice tight in my mind. He severed the arm of a sorcerer who tried to throw a curse at me. "Don't let the void take the driver's seat."

"It's loud," I gasped, ducking a sweep of green fire. "Valdus, it's so loud."

"Focus on me. Focus on the bond."

He grabbed the back of my tunic and hauled me out of the path of a collapsing column. Stone shattered where I had been standing a second ago.

We burst onto the mezzanine overlooking the Great Hall.

I skidded to a halt, my boots slipping on the blood-slicked marble. My hand flew to my mouth.

"Gods," I whispered.

The Great Hall was gone.

The massive oak doors had been blown inward. The courtyard beyond was a sea of green fire and writhing bodies. Hundreds of Fae poured through the breach, a tide of bone-armor and malice. The Sky Legion held the stairs, a thin line of silver against the green flood, but they were breaking.

Dragons roared outside, their fire illuminating the stained glass windows, but the anti-magic wards the Fae had erected were keeping them from strafing the impossible numbers inside.

"They brought a Siege-Breaker," Valdus said. His voice was cold, drained of all emotion.

He pointed.

In the center of the hall, surrounded by a ring of chanting sorcerers, stood a massive construct of flesh and iron. It looked like a giant made of corpses stitched together, wielding a hammer the size of a siege engine. Every time it swung, stone pulverized and men died.

"We can't win this," I said. The realization hit me like a physical blow. "Valdus, there are too many."

He looked at me. His face was streaked with soot and blood—some his, some mine, some theirs. The gold in his eyes had darkened to the color of old coins.

"We don't have to win," he said. "We just have to kill the Breaker."

"That thing is forty feet tall!"

"Size is a crutch." He tightened his grip on his sword. "It's slow. And it's maintaining the anti-air wards. If it falls, the dragons can burn the courtyard."

He grabbed my chin, forcing me to look at him. His fingers were hot, searing my skin.

"I'm going to drop on it," he said. "I need you to keep the sorcerers off my back."

"That's suicide."

"No. It's war."

He leaned in, his forehead pressing against mine. For a second, the screams below faded. There was just the smell of him—woodsmoke, blood, and the terrifying, musky scent of a male who had just claimed a mate and was about to kill for her.

"I am the Anchor," he whispered, the words vibrating against my skull. "I hold the line. You bring the fire. Do you understand?"

My heart hammered against my ribs, a frantic bird trapped in a cage. I wanted to beg him not to go. I wanted to drag him back into the library and hide until the world ended.

But looking at him—at the lethal set of his jaw, the grim acceptance in his eyes—I knew he wouldn't stop. He was the High Commander. He would spend his life to buy the Empire another hour of sunrise.

And I was the weapon he had chosen to yield.

"I understand," I said.

"Good girl."

The praise sparked a jolt of heat in my belly that had no business being there, tangling with the fear.

He stepped back. He vaulted onto the stone railing.

"Cover me!" he roared.

He jumped.

He plummeted forty feet into the chaos below.

I didn't watch him land. I moved.

I sprinted along the balcony, my daggers loose in my hands, searching for a vantage point. Below, Valdus hit the ground like a meteor. A shockwave of black fire blasted outward, clearing a circle in the enemy ranks.

He was a monster.

He moved through the Fae like a thresher through wheat, his greatsword carving a path toward the Siege-Breaker. But the sorcerers saw him.

Green lightning arced from the circle, aiming for his back.

"No!" I screamed.

I gathered the shadows. Not wisps. Not tendrils. I reached deep into the void that had terrified me in the library, the cold, hungry place that Vane had called the Bloodfire.

I pulled.

Darkness erupted from my hands. It flooded down from the balcony, a landslide of gloom. It slammed into the circle of sorcerers, blinding them, choking them.

Valdus didn't hesitate. He used the distraction. He lunged, driving his sword into the knee of the giant construct.

The beast roared, stumbling.

But there were too many enemies.

A group of Fae archers on the far stairs turned their bows toward me.

I saw the arrows coming. Time seemed to slow down. I tried to pull the shadows back to shield myself, but I had thrown too much. I was exposed.

Move!

But my legs felt like lead. The magic drain had sapped my speed.

An arrow struck the stone inches from my face. Another caught the sleeve of my tunic, pinning me to the doorframe.

I struggled, tearing the fabric.

A shadow fell over me.

Not magic. A person.

A Fae infiltrator had climbed the trellis. He landed silently on the balcony behind me.

I spun, dagger raised, but he was faster. He backhanded me.

The force of the blow sent me sprawling. My head cracked against the stone floor. Stars exploded in my vision.

I scrambled back, trying to regain my footing, but he was on me. He pinned my wrists to the ground, his weight crushing the air from my lungs. He didn't have a weapon. He had a collar. A thick band of iron glowing with runes.

"The King sends his regards," the Fae sneered, lowering the collar toward my neck.

Panic, cold and absolute, washed over me. Not for my life. For the silence. If that collar snapped shut, it would cut the bond. It would cut *him* off.

"Valdus!" I screamed. It wasn't a word; it was a psychic distress flare.

Below, in the pit of bodies, Valdus froze.

I felt it through the bond—the snap of his restraint. The calculated tactician vanished. The dragon took the leash in its teeth and snapped it.

He abandoned the Siege-Breaker. He abandoned the army.

He looked up.

His eyes were two suns.

He didn't run to the stairs. He didn't jump.

He *shifted*.

The air in the Great Hall shrieked as displacement magic tore it apart. One second, he was a man in armor. The next, he was a nightmare.

Scales of obsidian. Wings that spanned the width of the hall. A tail spiked with jagged bone.

The Black Dragon.

The roof of the Great Hall groaned as his massive form filled the space, scattering soldiers like toys.

He didn't roar. He inhaled.

The sound was the terrifying rush of a vacuum stealing all the oxygen from the room.

The Fae on top of me looked up, his eyes widening in horror. He scrambled off me, forgetting the collar, forgetting his mission.

Valdus released the breath.

It wasn't fire. It was a beam of pure, concentrated destruction.

It hit the balcony.

I scrambled backward, throwing myself into the alcove of a statue just as the world turned white. The heat was instantaneous. The Fae infiltrator didn't scream; he simply ceased to exist. The stone railing melted into slag.

The dragon hovered there, his massive head level with the balcony, smoke curling from his nostrils. His golden eye, the size of a shield, fixed on me.

Mine, the voice boomed in my head, loud enough to crack my skull. *Are you hurt?*

I shook my head, trembling, staring at the devastation. "No."

He had destroyed the structural support of the east wall to save me. The ceiling was beginning to sag.

Climb on, he commanded. He slammed a massive claw onto the balcony ledge, offering me a path to his neck.

I didn't hesitate. I ran.

I vaulted over the melting stone and grabbed the spur of bone at the base of his neck. The heat of his scales burned my palms, but I didn't care. I hauled myself up, settling into the hollow between his shoulder blades.

This was madness. We were abandoning the defensive line.

But as I pressed my chest against his warm, hard scales, the bond settled. The panic vanished, replaced by a cold, deadly clarity.

We weren't soldiers anymore. We were the calamity.

"Take them down," I whispered into the wind.

Valdus pushed off the wall, his wings shattering the stained glass as we burst out into the night sky, raining glass and fire down on the world below.

CHAPTER TWENTY

THE EMPTY LEASH

The wind screamed, a living thing tearing at the membranes of my wings, but the heat pressed against my spine was hotter.

Vea.

She clung to the base of my neck, her small body wedged between the spikes of obsidian bone. Through the bond, I felt her terror, cold and sharp as a splinter of ice. But beneath it, wrapped in the iron of her resolve, was a ferocity that matched the monster she rode.

We were not a general and his assassin anymore. We were a single instrument of ruin.

Hold on, I projected, my voice booming in the telepathic space between our skulls.

I folded my wings.

Gravity took us. We dropped from the smoke-choked sky like a judgment, plummeting toward the courtyard where the Fae lines were thickest. The ground rushed up—a mosaic of grey stone, green fire, and upturned, screaming faces.

I flared my wings at the last second. The air displacement hit the courtyard with the force of a bomb. Stone cracked. Fae soldiers were thrown like ragdolls against the citadel walls.

I hit the ground, claws gouging deep furrows into the granite to arrest the momentum.

Jump, I commanded.

Vea didn't hesitate. She vaulted from my back, rolling as she hit the pavement, daggers already flashing in the firelight.

I let the magic tear through me. The shift was always agony—breaking bones to reshape them, shrinking mountains of muscle into the dense, compact form of a man—but tonight I welcomed the pain. It was clarity.

I stood up, human skin knitting over dragon fire, and drew the greatsword from the shadowy rift where I kept it.

"On me!" I roared.

Vea was already moving. She ducked under a sweep of a bone-axe, hamstrung the wielder, and drove her blade upward into his throat. She was fast. Faster than she had been yesterday. My power was bleeding into her, speeding her reflexes, hardening her skin.

We fought back-to-back.

It was a dance of slaughter. I took the heavy blows, the crushing impacts of warhammers and the searing heat of sorcery, my shield of black magic absorbing the worst of it. She took the openings I created, a viper striking from the shadow of a mountain.

"Three on your left!" she shouted, her voice rough with smoke.

I spun, the greatsword singing a low, mournful note. I cleaved through chitin armor and pale flesh in a single stroke.

Through the bond, I felt her satisfaction—a grim, bloody thing. There was no fear in her now. Only the cold math of survival.

But the numbers were wrong.

For every Fae we killed, two more spilled over the breached walls. The courtyard was drowning in them. And in the center of the carnage, standing atop the fountain filled with dead cadets, was a figure cloaked in pale, shimmering robes.

A High Caster.

He didn't hold a weapon. He held a sphere of pulsing, sickly green light.

He wasn't looking at me. He was looking at Vea.

"Valdus!" Vea screamed.

I turned.

The Caster crushed the sphere.

The world turned green.

A shockwave of emerald fire rippled outward. It didn't burn; it pushed. It hit me like the fist of a god, lifting me off my feet and hurling me backward. I smashed into a stone pillar, the impact cracking my ribs.

I hit the ground, gasping, my sword skittering across the stones.

I scrambled up, ignoring the screaming protest of my chest.

"Vea!"

She was on the other side of the courtyard. The blast had thrown her toward the gatehouse. She was getting to her feet, shaking her head, blood dripping from her nose.

Between us, the air shimmered.

A wall of translucent green flame rose from the cracks in the stones. It shot upward, sealing off the gatehouse, bisecting the courtyard.

I ran.

I hit the barrier at full sprint.

It didn't yield.

The sound of my impact was swallowed by the magic. There was no crash. Just a wet hiss as the green fire seized my flesh.

Pain, white and absolute, tore up my arms.

I roared, incoherent with rage, and struck it again. The skin on my knuckles blistered and peeled away. I didn't care. I summoned the dragon's fire, coating my fists in the black void, and hammered against the wall.

Nothing.

It was an isolation ward. Ancient. Unbreakable by brute force.

"Vea!" I screamed her name, my hands pressing against the green glass, leaving smears of blood and charred skin.

She turned.

She saw me. She saw the wall.

She ran toward me, her eyes wide. She slammed her hands against the barrier on her side.

Our palms met, separated by three inches of magic.

And then the silence hit me.

The bond went dead.

It didn't snap. A snap implies a quick break. This was suffocation. It was as if someone had reached into my chest and scooped out the nerve center that connected me to the world. The constant hum of her presence, the heat of her emotions, the steady thrum of her life—gone.

I was hollowed out.

For a second, I couldn't breathe. The panic wasn't a thought; it was a physical failure of my lungs. I clawed at the barrier, my nails digging into the energy until they broke.

"No," I choked out. "No, no, no."

Vea knocked on the glass. She was shouting something, but the sound didn't carry. Her mouth formed my name. Her eyes were terrified.

Then, behind her, the shadows moved.

The Caster pointed a long, pale finger at her.

The Fae soldiers, who had been holding back, surged forward. Dozens of them. A tide of bone and malice, crashing toward the small, red-haired woman trapped against the green wall.

She spun around, her back hitting the barrier right where my hands were pressed.

"Turn around!" I bellowed, battering the wall with my shoulder. "Look at me! Vea!"

She didn't turn. She raised her daggers.

She fought.

I was forced to watch.

The first Fae reached her. She parried high, ducked low, and gutted him. But the second one clipped her shoulder with a mace. She stumbled.

A roar ripped from my throat—a sound that wasn't human. My dragon surfaced, clawing at the inside of my skin, demanding release. I poured everything I had into the barrier. Fire. Shadow. Brute strength.

The green wall didn't even flicker. It absorbed my rage and fed on it.

Vea was overwhelmed. There were too many blades. Too many hands.

A spearpoint caught her thigh. Blood—bright and red—sprayed onto the stones.

She fell to one knee.

My heart stopped. The world narrowed down to that splash of red.

A Fae soldier raised a heavy axe for the killing blow.

"Use it!" I screamed, smashing my forehead against the barrier, not caring that the skin split. "Burn them! Vea, burn them!"

She couldn't hear me.

But she felt the end coming.

She looked up. She didn't look at the axe. She turned her head, just slightly, and looked back at the wall. At me.

Her face was pale, streaked with grime. Her mouth was bleeding.

She mouthed two words.

I'm sorry.

Then, she closed her eyes.

She stopped fighting the enemy. She stopped fighting the container.

She let go.

The change wasn't subtle. It was a detonation.

The shadows around her feet didn't just lengthen; they stood up. They writhed like living oil, stripping the light from the air.

The Fae with the axe froze.

Vea opened her eyes.

They were pitch black. No iris. No sclera. Just two holes in reality where a soul used to be.

The axe fell.

Vea caught the blade.

She didn't catch the haft. She caught the steel edge with her bare hand.

Black blood—no, *liquid shadow*—welled up around her fingers, but she didn't flinch. She squeezed.

The steel shattered.

A shockwave of cold blasted outward from her body. It wasn't the heat of fire. It was the chill of the grave, the freeze of deep space. Frost spiderwebbed across the stones.

The Fae soldier stepped back, his mouth opening in a silent scream.

Vea stood up.

She didn't move like a cadet. She didn't move like an assassin. She drifted, suspended by the dark power pouring out of her skin.

"Burn," she whispered.

I heard it. Even through the soundproof barrier, I heard it. It vibrated in my teeth.

She threw her head back and screamed.

It wasn't a sound of pain. It was the sound of a seal breaking.

Black fire erupted from her chest.

It exploded outward in a catastrophic ring. It hit the Fae soldiers and they didn't burn—they *unmade*. One second they were flesh and bone; the next they were dust, scattering on the wind.

The Caster raised his hands, trying to shield himself.

The black fire ate his shield. Then it ate him.

I stopped hitting the wall. I slid down to my knees, my ruined hands pressing against the glass.

The fire swirled around her, a tornado of destruction. It consumed the bodies. It consumed the stone. It consumed the air.

She was doing it. She was fulfilling the prophecy.

She was burning the world to survive.

But as I watched the black flames lick at her skin, turning her pale flesh to ash-grey, I knew the truth.

She wasn't controlling it. It was eating her alive.

The separation had broken the Anchor. I wasn't there to ground the charge. I was just a spectator in the front row of the apocalypse.

Vea turned in the center of the inferno. She looked at me through the green distortion and the black fire.

She didn't recognize me.

The woman who had slept in my arms, who had fought me in the library, who had claimed my monster... she was gone.

The Bloodfire Queen stared back. And she was hungry.

Chapter Twenty-One

BEYOND THE SHADOWS REACH

The fire didn't burn. That was the lie they told in the songs.

The fire froze.

It started in the marrow of my bones, a creeping frost that turned my blood to slush and my breath to mist. The black flames I had summoned didn't roar; they whispered. They swirled around me in a silent, hungry vortex, licking at my skin, tasting the magic in my veins, deciding if I was fuel or master.

I was fuel.

I fell to my knees on the cracked stones of the courtyard. The world was a blur of shadows and grey ash. The bodies of the Fae soldiers I had unmade were gone, reduced to dust that coated my tongue with the taste of copper and rot.

The silence was the worst part. The screaming had stopped. The clash of steel had stopped. There was only the high-pitched ringing in my ears and the hollow thudding of a heart that was beating too slow.

Valdus.

The name was a ragged thought, a desperate clawing at the emptiness in my chest.

I lifted my head. The movement cost me everything. My neck felt too weak to support my skull.

The green wall was gone. The Caster was dead, his spell broken by the void I had unleashed.

And across the shattered remains of the courtyard, through the drifting smoke and the lingering tendrils of shadow, he was running.

He didn't look like a General. He looked like a catastrophe.

His armor was gone, shredded during the shift and the subsequent violence. He wore only tattered breeches that clung to thighs thick with muscle, stained dark with mud and blood. His chest—a broad expanse of bronze skin and old scars—heaved with the force of his breathing. Burns marked his arms where he had battered against the magic barrier, the skin raw and weeping gold-tinged blood.

He was terrifying. He was beautiful.

Even as my vision greyed at the edges, my traitorous body reacted to him. I drank him in, greedy for the sight of the only solid thing in a dissolving world. The sheer size of him was an assault on the senses. The way the cords of his neck strained as he sprinted, the heavy, lethal weight of his shoulders, the veins traversing his forearms like ridges on a map of violent territory. He was built for war, carved from granite and hate, yet he was running toward me with an expression that shattered my heart.

Panic.

Valdus, the butcher of nations, looked terrified.

"Vea!"

His voice was a raw scrape against the silence.

I tried to answer. I tried to say *I'm here, I'm alive,* but my throat was full of ash. I slumped forward, my hands hitting the cold stone.

He was there in a heartbeat.

He skidded to his knees in the dust, his hands hovering over me, afraid to touch. The black fire still clung to my skin, little wisps of shadow that snapped and hissed like vipers.

"Look at me," he commanded, his voice shaking. "Little Red, look at me."

I forced my eyes to focus. His face swam into view. The gold in his eyes was fractured, swirling with a storm of emotions I couldn't parse.

He reached out. He ignored the shadows. His large, calloused hands framed my face.

The contact sizzled.

Pain spiked through me, sharp and grounding. The cold retreated, chased back by the furnace heat of his skin.

"You're burning," I whispered. My voice sounded like dry leaves crushing.

"I heal," he rasped. His thumbs stroked my cheekbones, smearing soot and tears I didn't know I'd shed. "Gods, Vea. You stopped."

"I... stopped?"

"The fire. You pulled it back." He rested his forehead against mine, his breath mingling with mine. "You didn't let it take you."

I hadn't pulled it back. It had just run out of things to eat.

"Get up," he urged, his tone shifting, hardening back into the Commander. He slid one arm under my knees and the other around my back. "We have to move. The vanguard is down, but the main force—"

Clang.

The sound was heavy. Metallic. Final.

It came from above.

Valdus froze. His muscles turned to stone against me.

He didn't look up. He looked at me. And in that split second, I saw the realization hit him. The calculation. The checkmate.

"I'm sorry," he whispered.

"Valdus?"

He threw me.

He didn't hurt me, but the shove was forceful, sending me rolling across the stones, away from him, away from the center of the courtyard.

I tumbled to a stop, scraping my palms, and scrambled around just as the sky fell.

It wasn't a net. It was iron.

Thick, black chains plummeted from the darkness above. They didn't just fall; they struck like snakes. Heavy iron cuffs, forged with runes that glowed a sickly, pulsating purple, slammed into the stone where we had been kneeling a second ago.

But I wasn't there.

Valdus was.

One chain whipped around his left wrist. Another snatched his right ankle.

He roared—a sound of pure, primal fury—and yanked back. The muscles in his back bunched and writhed as he fought the metal. He was strong enough to tear a man in half, strong enough to wrestle a wyvern to the ground.

But he couldn't break this.

The runes flared.

Valdus stiffened. His roar cut off, strangled in his throat. He dropped to one knee, gasping, as if the air had been sucked out of the world.

Anti-magic.

The realization was a knife in my gut. They were draining him.

"Valdus!" I screamed, scrambling to my feet. My daggers were gone. My magic was empty. I ran toward him anyway.

"Stay back!" he bellowed. The command slammed into me, physical and heavy.

More chains dropped. They wrapped around his chest, his throat, his wings that he couldn't manifest. They dragged him down, forcing his face toward the stone.

From the shadows of the ruined gatehouse, figures emerged.

They weren't the mindless grunts in bone armor. These Fae moved with liquid grace, their armor polished silver, their faces beautiful and cruel.

At the center walked a tall male with hair like spun moonlight and eyes that looked like frozen ponds. He wore robes of deep indigo, unspotted by the carnage.

"Impressive," the Fae Lord said. His voice was smooth, cultured, and utterly repulsive. "We expected the Dragon to be difficult. We did not expect him to be... sentimental."

Valdus snarled, straining against the iron. The veins in his neck bulged, threatening to burst. "Touch her and I will dismantle this citadel brick by brick."

The Fae Lord smiled. It didn't reach his eyes.

"You are in no position to dismantle anything, General. That iron is forged in the deepest pits of the Void Courts. It drinks power. The more you struggle, the weaker you become."

The Lord turned his gaze to me.

I froze.

The look wasn't one of hatred. It was the look a butcher gives a prize hog. Appraisal. Hunger.

"And this," the Lord mused, stepping over a corpse to walk toward me. "The vessel. The Bloodfire Queen."

"She is nothing!" Valdus shouted, thrashing against the chains. The metal groaned, but held. "She is a gutter rat I picked up to warm my bed! Leave her alone!"

He was lying. He was trying to devalue me, to make me less of a target.

The Fae Lord laughed. "Oh, Valdus. We felt the detonation in the Void. A gutter rat does not unmake a High Caster. She is the weapon we have been promised."

He took another step toward me.

I backed up. My heel hit debris. I was cornered.

"Run, Vea," Valdus growled. His voice was low, laced with a vibration that rattled my teeth.

"I'm not leaving you," I said, my voice trembling.

"You are useless to me here," he snapped. Cruelty layered his tone, a desperate attempt to drive me away. "You are broken. You are empty. Get out of my sight."

"No."

The Fae Lord stopped ten feet from me. He extended a hand. Magic, cold and blue, gathered in his palm.

"We do not need her willing," the Lord said to his soldiers. "We only need her alive. The Dragon is the battery. If we have him, we can force the bond to feed her."

Valdus stopped fighting.

He went perfectly still.

He looked at the Fae Lord, then at me.

"You want the battery?" Valdus asked softly.

The Fae Lord arched a brow. "We have the battery."

"You have a man in chains," Valdus said. "You don't have the monster."

Valdus closed his eyes.

I felt it before I saw it. The bond—that silent, terrified connection between us—suddenly screamed.

He wasn't pulling power. He was pushing it.

He wasn't trying to break the chains. He was dumping his reserve. He was pouring every ounce of his magic, his life force, his soul, into the iron.

The runes on the cuffs flared brighter. Purple turned to blinding white.

"What is he doing?" one of the soldiers shouted.

"Overloading the dampeners," the Fae Lord hissed, stepping back. "Stop him!"

"Vea!" Valdus's eyes snapped open. They weren't gold anymore. They were white fire.

He looked at me. And in that look, there was no General. No monster. Just a man who had finally found something he loved more than war.

Command.

He didn't speak it aloud. He shoved it down the bond, a psychic hammer blow that bypassed my ears and struck my motor cortex.

RUN.

My body moved before my mind could protest. My legs turned, my muscles fired, and I sprinted toward the narrow servant's tunnel on the far side of the courtyard.

"I said stop him!" the Fae Lord shrieked.

"No!" I screamed, fighting my own legs. "Valdus, stop!"

I couldn't stop. The compulsion was absolute. He was using the Ancient Voice, the dragon's authority over its mate. It was a violation. It was a rescue.

Behind me, the world exploded.

Valdus released the energy.

It wasn't a fireball. It was a shockwave of pure kinetic force.

It blew the Fae soldiers off their feet. It cracked the foundation of the citadel. It sent the Fae Lord flying back into the darkness.

But the chains held.

The backlash hit Valdus.

I twisted my head as I reached the tunnel mouth, fighting the command just enough to look back.

Valdus arched back, his body seizing as the magic recoiled. Blood sprayed from his nose and mouth. He collapsed onto the stones, the white light fading from his eyes, leaving them dull and dark.

He didn't move.

"Get him!" the Fae Lord screamed from somewhere in the dust. "Get him before he wakes up!"

"Vea!"

A hand grabbed my arm. Rough. brutal.

I spun, lashes forming out of habit, but it was Kael. Valdus's lieutenant. His face was a mask of soot and blood, his eyes wild.

"Let me go!" I fought him, digging my heels into the mud. "They have him! They have him, Kael!"

"He bought you an exit!" Kael snarled, hauling me into the darkness of the tunnel. "Don't you dare waste it!"

"He's the Anchor!" I sobbed, the fight draining out of me as the horror set in. "If they take him... if he dies..."

"If he dies, you blow a crater in the continent," Kael said, dragging me deeper into the gloom. "Which is why we are getting you as far away from here as possible."

"No, no, no..."

I watched the patch of light at the end of the tunnel shrink.

Through the dust, I saw them swarm him.

Dozens of soldiers piled onto the prone, massive form of the High Commander. They beat him with the hafts of their spears. They kicked him. They tightened the chains until the iron bit into bone.

He didn't fight back. He was unconscious. Or dead.

The bond was silent. Not the silence of a held breath this time.

The silence of a severed limb.

Kael pulled me around a corner. The light vanished.

"Walk," Kael ordered, his voice cracking. "Walk, or I carry you."

I walked.

My feet moved over the damp stones of the sewer tunnel. My breath hitched in jagged, painful gasps.

I was alive. The Bloodfire was dormant. I was safe.

And all I could think about was the way he had looked at me before he used the Voice.

He hadn't looked at me like a weapon. He hadn't looked at me like a responsibility.

He had looked at me like I was the only thing worth burning for.

You want the battery?

I touched my chest, where the bond used to sing. It was just a dull, aching bruise now.

"I'm going to kill them," I whispered to the wet walls.

Kael didn't answer. He just kept marching, his grip on my arm bruising.

"I'm going to kill them all," I said louder. My voice stabilized. The grief was still there, vast and crushing, but something harder was crystallizing in the center of it.

Hatred.

Not for Valdus. Never for Valdus.

For the world that demanded a monster and then punished him for being one.

They thought they had captured the dragon. They thought they had won.

But they had made a mistake.

They had left the bomb on the outside.

And I was going to find a match.

Chapter Twenty-Two

The World for a Wound

The iron didn't just bind me; it drank.

Cold, hungry mouths pressed against my wrists and ankles, the rune-forged metal sucking the heat from my blood and the magic from my marrow. It was a violation deeper than any blade. It felt like being hollowed out with a rusty spoon, scraping away the dragon until only the man was left.

And the man was breaking.

I hung from the ceiling of the Black Hold's deepest cell, my toes barely brushing the stone floor. My shoulders screamed in their sockets. My chest was a roadmap of bruises and shallow cuts where the Fae had stripped my armor to see if I bled red or black.

Red. Always red when the dragon was caged.

A heavy, wet sound echoed in the darkness. My own blood, dripping from my nose to the floor. *Drip. Drip.*

"You are stubborn, General."

The voice was smooth, cultured, and coated in the slime of false civility. I forced my swollen eyelids open.

The Fae Lord stood before me. His robes were pristine indigo, a mockery of the filth and gore coating the dungeon walls. His eyes, those frozen ponds of indifference, studied me like a biologist dissecting a frog.

"I am merely... motivated," I rasped. My throat felt full of glass shards.

"Motivated by what?" The Lord stepped closer, careful not to step in the pool of my blood. "Loyalty to a dead King? Patriotism for an Empire that calls you a monster behind your back?"

"Spite," I said. "Pure spite."

He smiled, thin and sharp. "I think not. I think you are motivated by the little redhead currently fleeing into the sewers."

The mention of her hit me harder than the iron.

Vea.

I closed my eyes, seeking the bond. It was there, but it was faint, muffled by the anti-magic cuffs and the miles of stone between us. I couldn't feel her precise location, but I could feel her rage. It pulsed in the back of my skull, a hot, jagged rhythm. She wasn't running. She was planning.

Don't come back, I pushed the thought toward the connection, though I knew it wouldn't reach her. *Run, Little Red. Run until your legs give out.*

"She is a fascinated creature," the Fae Lord mused. "We felt the surge when she engaged the Bloodfire. It was... exquisite. Unrefined, yes, but the raw potential?" He inhaled deeply, as if savoring a fine wine. "She could unmake mountains."

"She'll unmake *you*," I growled.

"Perhaps. Or perhaps she will simply burn herself out before she gets the chance." He tilted his head. "That is the problem with the Bloodfire, isn't it? It consumes the vessel. Unless..."

He reached out, tapping a long, pale finger against the iron cuff on my wrist. The rune flared purple, sending a spike of agony up my arm that made my vision white out. I clenched my jaw until a tooth cracked, refusing to scream.

"Unless she has an Anchor," he finished softly. "A durable, regenerative battery to absorb the backlash."

The pain receded to a dull throb. I hung my head, breathing hard, sweat stinging my eyes.

"You want her," I said, my voice barely audible.

"We want the weapon. You are merely the safety catch." The Lord signaled to the shadows. Two soldiers in bone armor stepped forward. One held a heavy, heated rod. "Call her back, Valdus. Use the bond. Tell her you are suffering. Tell her to come save you."

"No."

"If you do not, we will peel the skin from your bones an inch at a time. And when you are screaming, we will make sure she hears it through the connection."

I looked up. I let the dragon bleed into my stare, even without the magic to back it up.

"Start peeling."

The Lord sighed, disappointed. He nodded to the soldier.

The hot iron sizzled against my ribs.

The smell of burning flesh filled the cell—acrid, sweet, sickening. The pain was blinding, a white-hot world that swallowed thought. But I didn't scream. I wouldn't give him that satisfaction. And more importantly, I wouldn't give Vea the signal.

I retreated.

I pulled my mind away from the cell, away from the smell of my own cooking meat, and went to the only place that mattered.

The library.

I saw her there, in my memory, from two nights ago.

She slept like she fought—curled tight, muscles coiled, a blade tucked somewhere in the tangle of sheets. Vea. My little assassin. My ruin.

Looking at her, barely five feet of scarred pale skin and defiance, the beast under my ribs clawed at its cage. My dragon roared to wrap around her, to bury her in obsidian scales until the world forgot she existed. The hunger was a physical weight, a constant, maddening ache to consume the fire waking in her blood. She thought she was the weapon, but she was the spark, and I was the powder keg waiting to blow.

I remembered tracing the air above her flame-red hair, my hand trembling not from weakness, but from the terrifying strain of restraint. Of *not* taking. The Fae courts encircled us, the skies were turning to poison, and the prophecy hung above her head like a guillotine.

I knew then what came next. I knew the price the bond demanded to keep her flame from burning out.

The fear that gripped me wasn't of death—it was of a world where she ceased to burn. If the cost of her survival was my breath, then I would gladly suffocate.

"He is not breaking," the soldier grunted, pulling the iron back.

The reality of the dungeon slammed back into me. My side was a ruin of blistered skin. My lungs heaved, struggling to pull air into a body that wanted to shut down.

"He is a dragon," the Lord said, sounding bored. "Pain is their currency. We need leverage."

He walked over to a small stone table in the corner and picked up a knife. Not a weapon of war—a delicate, silver thing.

"The bond transmits emotion," the Lord said, turning the knife in the torchlight. "Pain, yes. But also despair. Hopelessness."

He walked back to me. He didn't aim for my chest. He aimed for my face.

"If we cannot make you call her with words, we will make you call her with your silence. We will dismantle you until there is nothing left but the void. And she will feel that void, Valdus. She will feel you disappear."

He placed the tip of the blade against my cheekbone.

"Last chance. Summon the girl."

I looked him in the eye.

"You think I'm the battery?" I spat, blood splattering his pristine robes. "You think I'm the thing that keeps her safe?"

The Lord paused. "Are you not?"

A dark, broken laugh rattled in my chest.

"I'm the leash," I whispered. "I'm the only thing keeping her from burning this entire continent to ash. You didn't capture a hostage, you ignorant corpse-fucker. You removed the containment field."

The Lord frowned. "What are you talking about?"

"She isn't coming back to negotiate," I said, grinning through the agony. "She's coming back to end you. And now that I'm not there to hold the fire back... I hope you like the heat."

The Lord's eyes narrowed. He pressed the knife in. A line of fire traced down my jaw.

"We shall see."

He turned to the guard. "Leave him. Let the iron drain him to the brink of death. Then bring the healers. I want him awake when we start on the fingers."

They left. The heavy oak door slammed shut, sealing me in the dark.

The silence returned, heavier this time.

My body sagged against the chains. The adrenaline faded, leaving only the cold and the pain.

I checked the bond again.

It was quieter now. The rage had settled into something colder. Determination.

She was alive. She was free.

I rested my head against the cold iron of the chain.

Good girl, I thought, the words drifting into the darkness. *Don't come back for me, Vea. Burn them. Burn them all.*

But I knew her. I knew the stubborn set of her jaw and the loyalty she tried so hard to hide.

She would come back.

And when she did, I needed to be alive to catch her when she fell.

I focused on the pain. I let it sharpen me. I counted the drips of blood hitting the floor.

One.

Two.

Three.

I would endure. I would survive this hell. Because the alternative was leaving her alone in a world that wanted to eat her alive.

And as long as I had breath in my lungs, no one touched her.

Not even the gods.

Chapter Twenty-Three

The Lesson Ends in Ash

The sewer air tasted like copper and rot. It coated the back of my throat, a thick, oily film that made every gasp for oxygen a battle.

My boots splashed through sludge that reached my shins, but I couldn't feel the cold. I couldn't feel my legs. I was a puppet, my strings pulled by a single, thunderous command that still echoed in the hollowed-out scrape of my skull.

Run.

The compulsion was a physical weight, a massive hand shoving me forward into the dark when every fiber of my soul screamed to turn back.

"Keep moving," Kael grated out. His grip on my upper arm was a vice, his fingers digging into the bruise Valdus had left days ago.

"Stop," I rasped. The word tore my throat. "Kael, stop."

"He gave an order, Vea." Kael didn't look at me. He stared straight ahead into the gloom, his jaw set in a line of granite. "We honor it."

"He sacrificed himself!" I tried to dig my heels into the slick stones, but the Lieutenant was stronger, heavier. He dragged me through the muck like a sack of grain. "They have him. You saw the chains. They have him."

"And if we go back, they have you both." Kael kicked open a rusted grate, the screech of metal echoing like a dying bird. "Get in."

I looked at the narrow, dark opening.

The compulsion in my head flickered. The distance. The dampening stone. The magic Valdus had used to force me away was fraying at the edges.

I slammed my shoulder against the wet wall of the tunnel. "I am not leaving him to bleed."

Kael spun. The movement was so fast I barely tracked it. He slammed me back against the brick, his forearm pressing against my collarbone. It wasn't an attack; it was containment.

"He isn't bleeding, Vea," Kael hissed, his face inches from mine. In the faint, greenish light filtering from the grate above, he looked like a ghost. Soot streaked his cheeks. Blood—not his—matted his hairline. "Valdus doesn't bleed. He breaks. And right now, he is buying every second of your life with his own. Don't you dare throw that away because you want to play hero."

"I'm not playing."

My voice dropped. It wasn't the scrap-metal rasp of a terrified girl anymore. It was colder.

Shadows uncoiled from the corners of the tunnel. They didn't ask for permission. They slithered up my boots, wrapping around my calves, possessive and hungry.

Kael looked down. His eyes widened. He stepped back, releasing me as if I burned.

"Move," he ordered, though the authority in his voice fractured.

I pushed off the wall. The command to run was gone, replaced by a silence so loud it deafened me.

The bond.

I reached for it. I threw my mind against the mental wall where Valdus usually lived—the warm, stormy presence that had been in my head since the library.

Nothing.

Just a dull, throbbing ache. A phantom limb where my heart used to be.

"Where are we going?" I asked. I didn't recognize my own voice. It sounded hollow.

"Safe house. Sector Four. Old smuggler's den." Kael turned and squeezed through the grate.

I followed. Not because he ordered me, but because I needed a weapon, and I had left my daggers in the courtyard.

*

The safe house was a basement beneath a burned-out tannery. It smelled of curing leather and stale dust.

Kael barred the door with a heavy iron beam. He slumped against it, sliding down until he hit the dirt floor. He put his head in his hands. The adrenaline that had kept him upright was evaporating, leaving a shaking, broken soldier in its wake.

I didn't sit. I couldn't.

If I stopped moving, the reality would catch me.

I paced the small room. Four steps turn. Four steps turn.

"They had anti-magic chains," I said. It wasn't a question.

Kael looked up, his eyes bloodshot. "Void-iron. It drinks power. The more he fights, the weaker he gets."

"He surrendered." I picked up a rusted fire poker from the hearth, testing its weight. It was trash. "He could have leveled the courtyard. He stopped."

"He saw the Caster targeting you." Kael wiped a hand over his face, smearing the grime. "Valdus is a strategist, Vea. He calculated the odds. If he fought, you died. If he surrendered, you ran."

"He's an idiot." I gripped the iron poker until my knuckles turned white. "He thinks he's saving me."

"He *did* save you."

"For what?" I spun on him. "To live in a sewer? To hide while they skin him alive?"

Kael stood up slowly. He reached into his belt and pulled out a flask. He took a long pull, then offered it to me.

I slapped it out of his hand.

The tin flask clattered across the floor, spinning in the dust.

"Do not placate me," I warned. The shadows in the room deepened, leaching the light from the singular lantern hanging on the wall. "Tell me what happens next."

Kael stared at the flask. Then he looked at me, and for the first time, I saw pity in his gaze.

"Next, we wait."

"Wait?"

"The Fae Lord—Malikor—he doesn't want Valdus dead. Not yet. He wants the battery."

Battery. Valdus had said that. *You want the battery?*

"Explain," I demanded.

Kael sighed, a heavy, rattling sound. "The prophecy. The texts in the citadel... they weren't complete. Or maybe Valdus just didn't want you to know the fine print."

A cold knot formed in my stomach. "What fine print?"

"The Bloodfire isn't just a power, Vea. It's a parasite. It eats the host." Kael took a step toward me, his hands raised in surrender. "Historically, every Queen who awakened it burned out within a month. They turned to ash. Their bodies couldn't handle the output."

I looked at my hands. They were pale, trembling. I remembered the sensation in the courtyard—the cold fire eating the air, eating the stone. Eating *me.*

"Valdus knew," Kael said softly. "Why do you think he forced the bond? Why do you think he claimed you so violently? It wasn't just instinct. It was engineering."

My knees felt weak. I leaned against the rough wooden table. "He acted as a heat sink."

"An Anchor," Kael corrected. "The Dragon Riders bond to share strength. But a Mate bond... that shares life. He's massive, Vea. His magical reserves are an ocean compared to a normal caster's cup. He bound himself to you so the Bloodfire would draw from *him* instead of eating your soul."

The memory of the library crashed into me. The way he had devoured me, the desperation in his touch, the way he had poured his golden light into my shadows.

Die with me, I had said.

Mine, he had answered.

He hadn't just been claiming me. He had been saving me from my own biology.

"So if he dies..." I whispered.

"If he dies, the Anchor is gone," Kael said. "And the next time you use the fire, you won't stop burning."

The silence in the room stretched, heavy and suffocating.

I understood now. The surrender. The command. He hadn't just been protecting me from a Fae blade. He had been trying to get me far enough away that when they killed him, the magical backlash wouldn't liquefy my brain.

"He thinks I'm fragile," I said. The realization wasn't a sorrow; it was a spark.

"He thinks you are precious," Kael argued. "He loves you, you stupid girl."

"Love is a luxury for people who aren't being hunted." I pushed off the table.

I walked to the corner of the room where a cracked mirror hung on a nail.

I looked at myself.

The girl in the glass was a wreck. Red hair matted with dust. A bruise blooming purple across her cheekbone. Her tunic torn, revealing the pale skin of her shoulder where Valdus had bitten her.

But the eyes.

The eyes weren't the frightened green of the gutter rat who stole bread to survive.

They were rimmed in charcoal. The pupils were blown wide, swallowing the light.

I'm the leash, Valdus had shouted at the Fae Lord.

He was right. He was the restraint. He was the morality. He was the only thing standing between the world and the apocalypse I carried in my chest.

And they had taken him away.

They had cut the leash.

A laugh bubbled up in my throat. It was a dark, jagged thing.

"Kael," I said, not turning around.

"We rest for an hour," Kael said, moving to retrieve his flask. "Then we head for the Western Pass. The rebels will take us in."

"No."

Kael froze. "Excuse me?"

I turned.

The shadows in the room didn't just flicker this time. They snapped. The lantern glass exploded.

Distinct shards of glass chimed as they hit the floor, but the room didn't go dark.

A pale, cold light emanated from my skin. It wasn't the warm gold of the dragon. It was the negative space of a star.

"We aren't going to the Western Pass," I said. My voice was calm. It was the calm of a hurricane's eye.

Kael reached for the sword at his hip. Instinct. "Vea, control it. You're leaking."

"I'm not leaking. I'm waking up."

I walked toward him.

He was a Lieutenant of the Sky Legion. A killer trained in the pits of the Storm Citadel. He was six feet of muscle and steel.

He backed up.

"Valdus surrendered because he thought I was the liability," I said, step by step. "He thought he had to shield me. He forgot what I am."

"You're a danger to everyone including yourself," Kael snapped, though his hand trembled on his hilt. "If you flare up now, without him, you die. That's the math."

"Then the math is wrong."

I stopped in front of him. I reached out and took the flask from his hand. He didn't fight me.

I took a drink. The cheap whiskey burned going down. It felt good. It felt like fuel.

"Malikor made a mistake," I said, wiping my mouth. "He took the battery. But he left the bomb."

"Vea..."

"Valdus is in the Black Hold."

Kael nodded slowly. "The deepest dungeon. It's impregnable. The walls are three feet of granite shielding. The guards are elite."

"Good." I tossed the empty flask into the corner. "Then they won't be able to get out."

I closed my eyes.

I stopped fighting the void in my chest. I stopped trying to wall it off or suppress it like I had been taught. I let the mental barriers crumble.

Feed, I whispered to the dark.

The sensation was immediate. Cold hook-points of power sank into my blood. It hurt. It felt like freezing to death and burning alive simultaneously. Without Valdus to filter it, the magic was raw, jagged, and overwhelming.

But I didn't push it away. I grabbed it. I forced it to heel.

My head snapped back. A gasp tore from my lips as the power settled, heavy and dense, in my core.

When I opened my eyes, Kael was pressing his back against the door, his sword half-drawn.

"Your eyes," he whispered. "They're black."

"Gear up, Lieutenant," I said.

I walked to the pile of discarded weapons in the corner of the safe house. I found a pair of short swords—clunky, ill-balanced iron things. They weren't my daggers, and they certainly weren't Valdus's greatsword.

They would do.

I tested the edge of the blade against my thumb. A bead of blood welled up. It looked almost black in the strange light.

"We are going back," I stated.

"That is suicide," Kael argued, but the fight had left his voice. He was looking at me like I was a stranger. Or a predator he hadn't identified yet.

"No," I corrected him. I slid the swords into my belt. "Suicide is staying here and waiting for the bond to snap. Suicide is letting them break him."

I walked to the door.

Kael didn't move to block me. He stared at me, fear warring with awe in his expression.

"He told you to run," Kael said weaky.

"He told *Vea* to run," I said.

I placed my hand on the heavy iron bar blocking the door. I didn't lift it. I channeled the cold fire.

The iron turned grey. Then it turned to dust, crumbling to the floor in a heap of rust.

I kicked the door open. The night air rushed in, smelling of rain and distant smoke.

"Vea is gone," I said, stepping out into the shadows. "We are going to get my mate."

I looked back at him over my shoulder.

"Are you coming, or do I burn the city down by myself?"

Kael stared at the pile of dust that used to be a security bar. He sheathed his sword. He adjusted his armor. A grim, terrifying smile touched his lips—the smile of a man who realized he was no longer following a victim, but a calamity.

"The sewers won't work for a re-entry," Kael said, stepping up beside me. "They'll have watchers."

"We aren't using the sewers."

I looked toward the Citadel, rising like a black fang against the moonlit sky. I could feel him there. Faint. Suffering. Alive.

Hold on, I sent the thought into the dark, aiming it like an arrow. *I'm coming.*

"We're going through the front gate," I told Kael.

"There's an army at the front gate," he pointed out.

I lifted my hands. Black smoke began to curl from my fingertips, twisting into shapes that defied the wind.

"I know," I said. "I'm counting on it."

Chapter Twenty-Four

The Monster She Woke

Pain had a taste. It was copper, bile, and the distinct, cloying sweetness of rot.

I hung in the dark, the void-iron cuffs biting into my wrists until they scraped bone. My shoulders had dislocated hours ago—or maybe days. Time didn't exist in the Black Hold. There was only the rhythm of the torture. The sizzle of the iron. The snap of the whip. The silence of the bond where Vea used to be.

"Again," the Fae Lord whispered.

A soldier stepped forward. He held a blade heated to a dull cherry red. He pressed it against the ruin of my pectorals, right over the scar where a wyvern had gored me a decade ago.

My skin hissed. The smell of my own cooking flesh filled the small, damp cell.

I didn't scream. I didn't have the breath for it. I just stared at the stone floor, counting the drops of blood pooling between my toes.

One. Two. Three.

If I focused on the blood, I didn't have to think about the silence. I didn't have to think about the fact that I had cut the connection to the only thing that had ever made my heart beat for something other than war.

Run, Little Red.

The thought was a jagged shard of glass in my brain. I hoped she was halfway to the Western Pass. I hoped she was angry. Hate was a good fuel. It burned cleaner than grief.

"He is fading, my Lord," the soldier grunted, pulling the iron back.

"He is a dragon," Malikor's voice drifted from the shadows. "He does not fade. He waits."

Malikor grabbed my chin, forcing my head up. His fingers were cold, his face a mask of bored cruelty.

"Where is she, Valdus? The bond is quiet, but it is not broken. I can feel the hum. Where is the vessel?"

I spat a mouthful of blood onto his pristine indigo robes.

Malikor sighed. He backhanded me. The ring on his finger tore my lip.

"Stubborn," he muttered. "Bring the salt. We will wake him up properly."

The soldier turned to the table of instruments.

Then the world tilted.

It wasn't a sound at first. It was a vibration. The deep, tectonic groan of the earth protesting a violation. Dust sifted from the ceiling, coating my sweat-slicked skin in grey.

Malikor froze. "What was that?"

Thoom.

This time, the sound arrived. A dull, heavy impact that bypassed my ears and rattled my teeth. It felt like a mountain falling.

"Seismic activity?" the soldier asked, his hand hovering over a jar of salt.

"No," I rasped. The word was a rusty scrape against my throat. A dark, terrible amusement bubbled up in my chest, ignoring the agony of my ribs. "Not seismic."

Thoom.

Closer. Louder.

The heavy oak door of the cell sat at the end of a long corridor lined with granite. That corridor was currently screaming.

"Check the perimeter," Malikor ordered, his composure cracking. "The wards should have—"

The door didn't open. It evaporated.

There was no explosion. No fire. One second, the three inches of iron-bound oak were there; the next, they were dust, blowing inward on a wind that smelled of ozone and grave dirt.

The torches in the hallway died instantly, snatched away by a unnatural darkness.

But I could see. My dragon eyes adjusted to the gloom, picking out the shape standing in the threshold.

She was small. So small against the scale of the destruction she had just wrought. Her red hair was a beacon, but the rest of her was nightmare fuel. Shadows didn't just surround her; they bled from her skin, coating the floor, climbing the walls, dissolving the stone.

Vea.

My heart hammered a frantic rhythm against my bruised ribs. Terror and awe crashed into each other. I had told her to run. I had used the Voice to force her away.

And she had come back.

"Kill her!" Malikor shrieked, stumbling back.

The soldier lunged, drawing a short sword. He was fast, a veteran of the border wars.

He didn't make it three steps.

Vea didn't raise a hand. She didn't chant a spell. She just looked at him.

A tendril of shadow lashed out from her shadow, faster than a striking cobra. It wrapped around the soldier's neck. There was a wet, sickening crunch—the sound of a spine snapping like a dry twig.

The soldier dropped. He didn't hit the ground like a man; he hit it like a side of beef thrown onto a butcher's block. Dead weight. Useless meat.

Malikor backed into the corner, his face draining of color. He raised a hand, summoning green fire.

"I am a High Lord of the Winter Court!" he screamed. "You cannot—"

Vea walked into the room. Her boots made no sound on the stone. Her eyes were pitch black. No white. No iris. Just the void.

"You have something of mine," she said.

Her voice wasn't the voice of the girl who had stolen bread in the Lower Wards. It was the voice of a judge pronouncing a death sentence.

Malikor threw the fire.

Vea caught it.

She physically caught the bolt of magic in her hand. The green flames licked at her fingers, then turned black and died, consumed by the hunger living under her skin.

She flicked her wrist.

The shadows on the wall detached themselves. They swarmed Malikor. He didn't scream. He didn't have time. The darkness covered him, a living blanket of razor-edges and cold. There was a brief struggle, a tearing sound—like wet fabric ripping—and then silence.

When the shadows receded, there was nothing left of the High Lord but a stain on the granite.

Vea stood alone in the center of the cell.

She turned to me.

The silence stretched, heavy and suffocating.

I hung there, exposed. I was a ruin. My armor was gone, stripped away to leave me naked from the waist up, my breeches shredded and stained. My body—the weapon the Empire had spent millions of gold coins perfecting—was broken. Burns mapped my chest. Cuts crisscrossed my arms. My hands, the hands that had held her, were swollen and bloody, the fingers twisted at unnatural angles.

I wanted to look away. I wanted to hide the weakness. I was supposed to be the monster. I was supposed to be the shield. Seeing her look at me like this, helpless and strung up like a piece of meat, was a sharper agony than the iron.

"Vea," I croaked. "Go."

She didn't go. She stepped closer.

The blackness in her eyes receded, shrinking back until the green returned. But it wasn't the soft green of spring grass. It was the hard, cold green of emeralds under winter ice.

She stopped inches from me. She didn't look at my face.

Her gaze raked over me, slow and deliberate. It started at my bare feet, traveled up the scarred, blood-streaked expanse of my legs, and lingered on the heavy muscles of my thighs. She traced the lines of my hips, the V-taper of my torso, ignoring the burns to appreciate the unforgiving width of my shoulders.

There was no pity in her eyes. There was no horror.

There was hunger.

Her eyes darkened as they fixed on the span of my chest, rising and falling with shallow breaths. She looked at the blood on my skin not as a wound, but as a decoration. She looked at the brute, massive reality of my body like I was a fortress she intended to conquer. It was a look of pure, unadulterated thirst, possessive and primal. She didn't care that I was broken; she only cared that I was *hers*.

A jolt of arousal kicked through me, violent and inappropriate. My dragon roared its approval from the depths of my mind, rattling the cage of my exhaustion. *Let her look. Let her claim.*

"You didn't run," I whispered.

"No." She reached out. Her hand, small and pale, landed on my chest, right over my heart. The contact scalded. "I found a match."

"They'll kill you. The army..."

"The army is busy burning."

She looked up at the chains holding my wrists. Her jaw set.

"Hold on," she ordered.

She didn't use a key. She grabbed the void-iron cuff on my left wrist with her bare hand.

"Vea, don't! It drains—"

"Burn," she commanded.

Black fire erupted from her grip. It flowed into the iron. The metal screeched, turning white-hot, then grey, then dust.

The cuff crumbled.

Gravity took me.

I fell forward, my legs too numb to catch me. I braced for the impact, for the shattering of bone against stone.

I didn't hit the floor.

Shadows surged up from the ground, solidifying instantly. They weren't wisps; they were thick, muscular tendrils of darkness that wrapped around my chest and waist, catching my massive weight with terrifying ease. They held me suspended, gentle but firm, acting as the strength I no longer possessed.

Vea dissolved the other cuff.

The shadows accepted my full weight, lowering me slowly until my knees touched the ground.

I slumped forward, my forehead resting against her stomach. I was shaking. The anti-magic field was gone, and the sudden rush of the bond returning was overwhelming. It flooded my senses—her scent (rain and ozone), her heat, her rage.

"I told you to leave," I mumbled into her tunic. "I used the Voice."

"I know." Her fingers threaded through my matted hair, scratching lightly against my scalp. "Don't ever do it again."

"I had to save you."

"You don't get to save me by dying, Valdus." She gripped my hair, forcing my head back until I looked at her. "The prophecy says I burn the world. It doesn't say I do it alone."

I looked into her face. The gutter rat was gone. The frightened girl who had tried to stab me in the stable was gone.

This was a Queen. A Queen of ash and bone.

And she was right. I hadn't saved her. I had simply unleashed her.

"Can you walk?" she asked.

"If I say no?"

"Then I carry you." And looking at the shadows writhing around her legs, I knew she could.

I gritted my teeth. I forced air into my lungs. I called on the reserve of power that was slowly trickling back into my veins now that the iron was gone.

"I can walk."

I pushed myself up. It was ugly. I swayed, my vision swimming.

Vea wrapped her arm around my waist. She barely reached my ribcage, but she felt like a pillar of granite.

"Lean on me," she said.

I leaned.

We moved toward the shattered doorway. The corridor beyond was empty. The guards were either dead or smart enough to run.

"Kael?" I asked.

" waiting at the main gate. With my swords."

I let out a breath that was half-laugh, half-sob. "You brought swords."

"I'm learning."

We stepped over the pile of dust that used to be a High Lord.

As we emerged from the Black Hold into the courtyard, the sky was red. Not from the sunset. From the city.

The Lower Wards were on fire. The Citadel walls were breached. Dragons—my dragons—were circling overhead, confused, leaderless, roaring at the smoke.

I looked at the chaos. I looked at the woman beside me, who had walked into the mouth of hell and torn its throat out to get me back.

The leash was gone. The containment was broken.

And as I felt the first flicker of my own fire return, hot and golden and deadly, I realized I didn't want to put it back.

"They're going to come for us," I said, watching a squadron of Fae soldiers gathering on the ramparts.

Vea looked at them. Her eyes flashed black again. The shadows at her feet lengthened, sharpening into blades.

"Let them come," she said.

I looked at her—my ruin, my salvation, my mate. The obsession that had driven me to surrender was nothing compared to the dark, violent devotion blooming in my chest now.

I shifted my weight, freeing my hand to grip her shoulder. Blood slicked my skin, but I held on.

"Burn them all, Little Red," I whispered.

She smiled. It was the most terrifying thing I had ever seen.

"We will."

Chapter Twenty-Five

The Monster She Calls Home

The silence of the Storm Citadel was a liar.

It pretended to be peace. It pretended the stone walls weren't soaked in the blood of the Winter Court, that the courtyard wasn't a graveyard of ash and bone-armor. I sat on the edge of the massive four-poster bed in the High Commander's quarters—*my* quarters now, by right of conquest—and stared at the woman sleeping in the center of the mattress.

Vea.

She looked small against the dark fur throws. Too small to be the reason the Empire was currently tearing itself apart in panic. Her flame-red hair spilled across the pillows like spilled wine, vibrant against the charcoal sheets. One of her hands, callous and scarred, rested near her face, the fingers curled loosely as if still gripping a dagger.

My dragon coiled tight in my chest, a beast sated yet starving.

I wanted to wake her. The urge was a physical pain, a constant ache in my marrow. I wanted to crush her against me until I couldn't tell where my obsidian scales ended and her pale skin began. I wanted to drag her back into the dark, cover her with my body, and snarl at anything that dared to breathe the same air.

Mine.

The word was a heavy stone in my gut.

I reached out, my hand trembling. Not from weakness—though the torture in the Black Hold had left its marks—but from the terrifying strain of restraint. My thumb brushed the hollow of her throat. Her pulse beat there, steady and strong.

Thump-thump. Thump-thump.

A drum of war against the silence.

She stirred. Her lashes fluttered, and then those eyes opened.

They weren't the pitch-black void of the Bloodfire anymore. They were green. Sharp, intelligent, dangerous green.

"You're staring," she rasped, her voice thick with sleep.

"I'm keeping watch."

"The door is barred, Valdus. And you killed everyone who knows how to pick the lock."

She pushed herself up, the fur throw slipping down to reveal the bandages wrapping her torso. My chest tightened. I had done that. I hadn't been there to Anchor her, and the fire had eaten at her ribs.

"Malikor is dead," I said, the name tasting like ash. "But the Void Courts won't let a High Lord's death go unanswered."

Vea looked at me. She didn't offer comfort. She didn't tell me it would be okay. She reached out and wrapped her hand around my wrist, her fingers spanning the thick bone, possessive and firm.

"Good," she said. "I'm still hungry."

A dark, twisted pride bloomed in my chest.

I leaned down, pressing my forehead against hers. The bond between us—that psychic tether that had been muffled by iron and distance—roared to life. It wasn't a trickle anymore. It was a river of fire and shadow, flowing from her to me and back again.

"Get up, Little Red," I whispered against her mouth. "We have a kingdom to burn."

*

SIX MONTHS LATER

The wind howling over the Western Peaks carried the scent of snow and sulfur.

I stood on the battlements of the Storm Citadel, the stone rough under my gloved hands. The fortress had changed. The banners of the Empire, with their golden dragons on blue fields, were gone. In their place hung heavy tapestries of black and crimson—the colors of the rebellion. The colors of the Bloodfire Queen.

Below, in the training pits where Vea had once been beaten bloody by cadets twice her size, an army drilled.

They weren't the polished legions of the King. They were a motley collection of deserters, mercenaries, and Low Ward gutter-rats who had heard the stories. They had heard that the monster of the Empire had broken his leash. They had heard that a girl with fire in her veins had killed a High Lord of the Fae.

They didn't come for gold. They came for revenge.

"The formations are sloppy."

I didn't turn. I felt her approach before I heard her. The bond warmed, a distinct sensation of heat rising at the base of my skull.

Vea stepped up beside me. She wore black leather armor, reinforced with dragon scales I had shed during the transition. A cloak of deep red wool hung from her shoulders, pinned with a brooch of obsidian.

She looked lethal. She looked like royalty.

"They're angry," I said, watching a massive deserter drive a spear through a dummy. "Anger makes men sloppy. But it makes them brave."

"Brave gets you killed," she countered. "Smart gets you home."

She leaned her elbows on the stone, looking out over the valley. The scars on her face had faded to silvery lines, badges of honor from the night we took the Citadel.

"The scouts returned," she said softly.

I went still. "And?"

"The King is moving the Third Legion. General Kaelen is marching on the pass."

Kaelen. My replacement. A man who followed orders as blindly as I once had.

"He brings twenty thousand," Vea continued, her voice devoid of fear.

"We have five," I noted.

"Five thousand soldiers. Three wyverns." She turned her head, looking up at me. A slow, terrifying smile curved her lips. "And us."

I looked down at her. Six months ago, the thought of an army marching on us would have sent me into a spiral of protective panic. I would have tried to hide her. I would have tried to bear the weight alone.

But we had broken that wheel in the dungeon.

"Does he know?" I asked.

"About the Anchor?" She shook her head. "No. The Empire still thinks you're just a traitorous General and I'm a sorcery accident waiting to happen. They think if they kill you, I'll burn out. They think if they corner me, I'll explode."

"They're half right."

I turned, putting my back to the valley, and pulled her into me. My hands spanned her waist, feeling the solid muscle beneath the leather. She didn't melt into me; she braced against me, strength meeting strength.

"I missed you this morning," I murmured, brushing a stray lock of red hair from her forehead.

"War council ran late. Lord Vane thinks we should negotiate with the Southern Duchies."

"Lord Vane is a coward who smells the rot in the crown and wants to secure his own lands."

"I know." Her eyes flashed. "I told him if he mentioned a treaty again, I'd feed him to your dragon."

A low laugh rumbled in my chest. "He'd give the beast indigestion."

"Valdus." Her tone dropped. The playfulness vanished, replaced by the steel that ruled this fortress. "If Kaelen breaches the pass... the magic dampeners won't hold. I'll have to fully engage."

She was asking me if I was ready.

Engaging the Bloodfire wasn't just physical for her; it was a drain on me. I became the battery, the ground wire for a voltage that should strip flesh from bone. It hurt. It felt like holding a star in my bare hands.

And I lived for it.

"Let him breach," I said, my voice rough. "Let him bring his twenty thousand. Let him bring the King himself."

I slid my hand up her spine, gripping the back of her neck, my thumb pressing into the soft skin beneath her ear.

"You draw from me, Vea. Take everything. If my heart stops, restart it. If my bones crack, let them. But do not hold back."

Her pupils dilated, swallowing the green. The hunger was there, the darkness that frightened everyone in this castle except me.

"You're a masochist," she whispered.

"I'm yours."

I kissed her. It wasn't gentle. It was a collision of teeth and desperation, a sealing of the pact we had made in blood. I tasted the coffee on her tongue and the violence in her soul. I deepened it, my tongue sweeping her mouth, reclaiming the territory I had fought the gods to keep.

She groaned, a low sound in her throat, and bit my lower lip. Hard. Usefully hard. The sharp sting of pain grounded me.

"The Council is waiting," she said against my mouth, breathless.

"Fuck the Council."

"We have to plan the defense."

I pulled back, just an inch, so I could look her in the eye.

"There is no defense, Little Red. We aren't defending anything."

I looked over her shoulder, toward the pass where the dust of the King's army would soon sully the horizon.

"We are the invasion."

*

The Great Hall of the Storm Citadel was a cavern of shadows and flickering torchlight.

A massive table of black iron dominates the center of the room. Around it sat the architects of our rebellion: mercenary captains with scars older than the King, disillusioned sorcerers in tattered robes, and Lieutenant Kael, who stood at the head of the table, looking tired.

Vea sat at the head. The obsidian throne was too big for her frame, but she filled it with sheer presence. She didn't slouch. She didn't fidget. She sat with the stillness of a predator waiting for movement.

I stood at her right hand. Always at her right.

I didn't sit. The monster didn't sit at the table; the monster guarded the door. Or in my case, the monster guarded the Queen.

"The supply lines from the south are cut," a mercenary named Jarek shouted, slamming his fist onto the iron. "If we don't secure grain before winter, we starve before the Legion even gets here."

"We have reserves," Kael said calmly. "Enough for three months."

"And then what?" Jarek sneered. He looked at Vea. "We are following a girl and a disgraced General into a tomb. We need allies. The Winter Court—"

The temperature in the room dropped ten degrees.

Vea didn't raise her voice. She didn't even blink.

"The Winter Court," she said, her voice cutting through the shouting like a razor through silk, "is the reason half of you are orphans. You want to ask them for bread?"

"I want to live!" Jarek stood up. He was a big man, broad and stupid. "We cannot fight the Empire and the Fae alone. We need to leverage the General. Send him to the capital. Offer terms."

The room went silent.

Every eye turned to me.

I didn't move. I leaned against the stone pillar behind the throne, my arms crossed over my chest. I watched Jarek with the disinterested curiosity of a wolf watching a rabbit limp.

"You want to trade me," I said softy.

Jarek swallowed but held his ground. "You are the High Commander. You know their strategies. You are valuable."

"I am not the Commander," I corrected him. I pushed off the pillar. The sound of my boots on the stone was the only noise in the hall.

I walked toward Jarek. He flinched, his hand dropping to the hilt of his sword.

"I am a weapon," I said, stopping a foot from him. I towered over him. I let the dragon bleed into my eyes—liquid gold drowning the white. "And weapons do not negotiate. Weapons do not offer terms."

I turned my head, looking back at Vea.

She watched me. Her face was impassive, but I felt the hum of approval in the bond. *He's crossing the line,* she sent silently. *Remind him who holds the leash.*

I looked back at Jarek.

"You think you are following a girl?" I asked, lowering my voice until the captains had to lean in to hear. "You think she is some political figurehead you can maneuver?"

I laughed. It was a dark, dry sound.

"You are standing in the blast radius of a god," I told the room. "The only reason you aren't ash right now is because she likes you. Do not give her a reason to change her mind."

Jarek sat down. He looked pale.

Vea stood up.

"Valdus is right," she said. "We don't trade. We don't beg."

She walked to the large map of the continent spread across the iron table. She picked up a dagger and stabbed it into the location marking the Capital.

"The Third Legion is coming for us," she said. "Let them come. They are bringing us our supplies. They are bringing us our winter grain. And they are bringing us their armor."

She looked up, her eyes scanning the faces of the captains.

"We march at dawn to meet them in the pass. Dismissed."

The captains scrambled to leave. They moved fast, eager to be out of the room, eager to be away from the heavy gravity of the couple at the head of the table.

Kael lingered for a moment, looking at us. He shook his head, a small, weary smile touching his lips, and followed them out.

The heavy doors groaned shut.

Vea slumped. Just a fraction. The mask of the Queen slipped, revealing the exhausted woman beneath.

"Jarek is going to be a problem," she muttered, rubbing her temples.

"I can kill him," I offered. "Quickly. Quietly."

"No." She sighed. "We need his men. His heavy infantry is the only thing that can hold a shield wall against a cavalry charge."

She looked at me. "Besides, you scared the piss out of him. He'll fall in line."

I walked over to her. I didn't stop until my thighs bumped against the arm of her throne.

"You were magnificent," I said.

She peered up at me, tilting her head back against the obsidian. "I was terrified. We're outnumbered four to one, Valdus."

"Numbers are for people who can't melt stone."

I reached down, gripping the arms of the throne, caging her in. The proximity was a drug. The scent of her fear—faint, but there—mixed with her determination. It called to everything dark inside me.

"Take me to bed," she said. It wasn't a request.

"The war planning..."

"Can wait." She grabbed the lapels of my tunic and pulled. "I need to not be a Queen for an hour. I need..."

She didn't finish the sentence. She didn't have to.

I needed it too. After the politics, after the noise, I needed the primal truth of us.

I scooped her up. She weighed nothing in my arms, a feather made of lead and fire. She wrapped her legs around my waist, burying her face in the crook of my neck.

I carried her out of the hall, not toward the bedroom, but toward the balcony that overlooked the drop.

The night air was freezing. It bit at our skin as I set her down on the wide stone railing. It was reckless. A hundred-foot drop to the jagged rocks below.

She didn't flinch. She gripped my shoulders, her eyes wide and dark.

"Right here," she breathed.

I didn't hesitate. I stepped between her knees, pushing the heavy leather skirt up her thighs. My hands found her skin—hot, soft, alive. The contrast between the freezing wind and her heat made my head spin.

I kissed her, swallowing her gasp. My hands weren't gentle. They were bruising, claiming, desperate. I needed to feel every inch of her to know she was still here, still mine.

"Tell me," she demanded, her nails digging into my neck. "Tell me we survive this."

I lifted her hips, pressing her against me, letting her feel the hard ridge of my desire, the undeniable proof of life in a grim world.

"We don't just survive," I growled against her throat.

I looked out over her shoulder, past the battlements, past the sleeping army, to the dark horizon where the enemy fires were just beginning to flicker like distant stars.

They were coming. The King. The Legion. The world.

They were coming to put the monster back in his cage and the fire back in the bottle.

I looked back at Vea. My Little Red. My apocalypse.

"We are going to rewrite the map," I promised her.

The wind tore at our clothes, screaming of winter and war. But in the circle of my arms, she was warm. She was the only thing that mattered.

"Let them come," I whispered into the dark. "Let them all come. We will burn them all."